# THE MILLENNIUM SOLDIER

## The Ancient Ones

## Book One

# THE MILLENNIUM SOLDIER

## The Ancient Ones

### Book One

*A "Sci-fi" thriller that
moves with warp speed
through the galaxy of a future
where good and evil  stand
in stark contrast.*

**Brevia Publishing Co.
101 W 75th Pl
Merrillville, IN 46410**

*http://millenniumsoldier.com*

***ISBN 978-0-9628531-6-6***

## Introduction

During the thousand years called in the Holy Scriptures, The Millennium, the earth became a planet of peace and industry. The Ancient Texts tell of the imprisonment of an evil being called Lucifer for 1000 years. During this thousand years, one called Messiah ruled.

There were no more wars. No diseases afflicted the inhabitants of Earth in this time. There were no cancers, no heart disease, and no illness. The life expectancy of humans rose to hundreds of years. There was order and tranquility. And, for a millennium, peace enveloped the world. There was no crime. Beings that had once died, called "resurrected" humans, ruled the planet with Messiah. Their minds and bodies, no longer hindered by the human limitations of mortals, assisted in the administration of government on the planet Earth.

During this time technological breakthroughs are made and enormous discoveries are made in all the sciences, and many incredible inventions take place, including unlimited space travel. Mankind embraces traveling throughout the universe. As disease is conquered by the new discoveries, and the life span of the average human increases to levels akin to spans attested to in the beginning of mankind's history, overpopulation becomes a problem. Millions opt to leave earth for adventure and a new life on other worlds.

*And then the thousand years came to an end.*

Lucifer is set free as foretold and decreed by the Holy Writ. On earth, violence erupts once more, fueled by the malignancy of Lucifer and his spawn of evil beings created by him to aid in his destruction of humanity. Wars break out amongst all nations and stretches its tentacles to other worlds. The stage is being set for Armageddon—that final battle between good and evil.

The universe has become a murky legion of worlds loosely aligned, populated by humans from earth and aliens whose origins are often unknown. One such race is the Crs'tings, an alien race whose origins seem to be of Earth, but who have learned the art of cloning the human race. There is some evidence their origins were creations of that evil being called Lucifer. Many strange and sinister forces, evil humans and non-humans, align themselves with Lucifer for the coming war.

It is a war against all humanity.

It is a war against heaven itself.

This is the story of an unusual man named Cubal—a warrior trained in an ancient form of combat known as D'vru. He is a designed human—a creation of DNA genetic manipulation. He was bred for war, but after the war years ended, he wandered the universe, a warrior with no wars to fight.

*Until now.*

Cubal is the ultimate soldier, and Lucifer wants to use him in the ultimate ware. It is a war against God and humanity.

Messiah wants to use him, too.

But, a Warrior of D'vru believes in neither gods nor devils.

*Yet.*

# Table of Contents

# Chapter 1

*"Beware measuring the strength of the life force of an enemy by his weakness, even if you truly know that weakness, for some will have strength in their weakness." - D'VRU, BOOK ONE: The Force of Life*

The jungle air was heavy with the scent of the Bora tiger. Soft, velvet sounds of the night moved without form through the tangled brush and thick vegetation. The moons of Vega I sprayed blue lance-like beams through the tree-tops, illuminating the night with its blue-black, eerie hue. The pale white skin of the Bora tiger stood in stark contrast against the deep shadows. Its massive head was as unmoving as the granite boulder it stood upon, surveying the small clearing below.

The creature's reddish-brown eyes locked upon its prey: a lone, two-legged creature sitting cross-legged on the ground below, his shoulders covered in a dark cape. The big cat crouched, the heavy muscles rippling with power, gathering tension. The long velvety tail of the Bora tiger stopped its snake-like movements and rested silently on the rock. The tiger's head lowered, and then suddenly, the big cat unleashed the power that had trembled in check. It leaped from the rock straight out into the air and downward toward the quiet, still figure.

Hidden nearby, watching the scene play out, stood a large man, his skin tone a light mahogany, with a wide muscular frame. His hair lay close to his skull in heavy, copper-colored ringlets. Golden chains lay against his bare chest, and a heavy, silver medallion hung from one of the chains. His arms were covered with silky brown hair, and his face was clean with the shine of strength and health. Jules carried a slim, silvery spear. Its point was as fine as a needle, and it was not merely a boast by the big man that he could drive the spear through five men.

Jules stood frozen in place in the small grove of trees just at the edge of a clearing, observing one of the strangest sights he'd ever seen. He'd spotted a strange man clad in a black cloak early in the day and had followed him from the river to this clearing. He'd watched as the man had performed what appeared to be rituals unlike anything Jules had ever seen, for several hours. The stranger had made curious movements with his hands, and made steps that appeared to be a kind of dance. At one point, the stranger had come to a complete stop to all movements, freezing in place for nearly a half hour, without so much as a muscle quivering. Finally, the figure had sunk to the ground cross-legged and sat unmoving, his hands on his knees, his head looking down at the ground. Jules glanced at the moons and knew the time had been four hours for the twins had passed in the sky twice.

Jules had also seen the silent moves of the stalking, Bora tiger. The creature had moved into position on an outcropping of rock just above the quiet, unmoving man Jules had been watching. Jules fingered his spear. He had no relish for a fight with the tiger. It was the strongest and fastest of all the creatures in the jungle, but even more, it was almost impossible to kill. Jules had passed his spear deep into more than one Bora tiger in his time, and as yet, had been unable to slay one.

Years ago, he'd hunted the Bora with seven other men from his village. Each one of them had driven a spear into the creature—seven spears all firmly driven deep—only to watch in astonishment as the big cat somehow caused the spears to be ejected from its body with no seeming harm to it. It was on that day that he suddenly believed the tales of the old men. They'd always said that the Bora tiger can only be killed by light and heat.

He watched, unable to assist, even to shout a warning, knowing that his warning would be futile because the speed of the big cat was too great. Jules also did not want to alert the cat to his own presence. He stood silent, waiting for the white-skinned death to strike the stranger. He would move quietly away from the white death while it was feeding.

Jules stood absolutely still, his eyes absorbing the drama in morbid fascination as the tiger leaped with a surge of its rope-like muscles, its huge white torso spread out, front paws stretched toward its prey, with its bluish talons extended, ready to rip and tear.

As the big cat leaped at its prey, Jules sucked air inwards in sudden surprise. The sitting figure moved from his position with a speed that did not seem possible for any man. One moment the man was sitting, and suddenly, the man was nearly ten feet from where he'd been sitting. The black cloak covering the man now fell from his shoulders, and Jules saw a lithe, yet powerful looking upper torso, clad in a dark, loose fitting shirt. The hands of the stranger moved before him in a circular pattern, weaving back and forth as though searching, feeling things unseen. The tiger landed where the man had been sitting and whirled around, its speed astonishing for its size.

Jules marveled, for he knew the man could not have heard the silent death leap of the huge tiger. No prey ever heard the stalk or the leap of the Bora tiger. Yet, the stranger had somehow known, and now was standing several feet away, his hands still moving slowly before him, still feeling the air, as though he were searching for something invisible.

A low growl of displeasure sounded from the beast. Never before had a prey leaped from its grasp in this manner. Always, prey that somehow managed to evade his initial attack, had attempted to flee, and the beast simply ran it down and killed it. This strange creature did not run, but stood facing him. The tiger did not think of it in human terms, but it sensed that this creature had no fear of him. Jules saw a faint smile flicker across the man's face and disappear. Man and beast stood for seconds staring at one another.

The Bora tiger lashed its tail back and forth. He'd frozen in his position when he'd landed, something completely uncommon for him. The tiger's mind was not a thing which reasoned as a human. The beast's mind was one that sent constant messages, images and alerts. The message he'd gotten was caution. Something strange

3

radiated from the creature standing near him, and it disturbed the big cat. The tiger sensed danger in the prey. Still, there was no fear in the beast, only caution as it advanced slowly toward the still figure.

Jules watched, completely absorbed in the drama unfolding before his eyes. Somehow the man had been able to detect the tiger and had moved with a speed that Jules would have said, before today, was impossible. The complete absence of fear was apparent in the stranger, and Jules knew then that the man was not of this world, for all in his world feared the Bora tiger. Even Jules. He licked his lips as the big animal crept forward, its body going lower and lower as it advanced, bunching its huge muscles together as it readied itself for the kill.

Again, the tiger leaped. This time, the stranger did not move aside, but instead, leaped directly at the oncoming creature, seemingly in the same instant the big cat leaped. Jules gasped in disbelief. Never had he seen a man leap so far, nor so high, and this without even a short run. The stranger had simply taken two steps and leaped into the air at the oncoming beast. He saw the stranger moving, almost as though in slow motion, then knew that the hands and feet of the man were moving much faster than his eye could follow, for he could see the blur of movement. The two met in mid-air, and instantly there was an explosion of violent movement and ear-shattering screams and snarls from the tiger. There was no sound from the stranger.

The forms separated even as they were falling to the ground. The huge tiger landed without its usual grace and exquisite balance. It hit the ground hard, landing on its side, then rolled once and staggered to its feet, visibly shaken, but not from the fall. The stranger stood nearby, his arms folded, intently watching the creature. A long minute passed as they stared at each other, then the great beast shook itself, turned slowly and padded toward the thick brush. It reached the edge of the trees, stopped and looked back at the strange creature staring so intently at him. The animal growled a low, gurgling sound, then disappeared into the jungle.

"You may come out now." The words were in his own language and came from the stranger.

The voice was commanding, yet not threatening. Jules saw the stranger staring at his hiding place, and suddenly felt afraid. It was as though he could feel the strange man's eyes upon him. He still did not comprehend what he'd just witnessed, for never in the  history of his world had a man met and defeated a Bora tiger without fire or light. The only weapon Jules had seen was the man himself.

"Come out. I will not harm you." The voice was gentler now and persuasive.

Jules stepped out into the clearing, his spear held loosely. Only those who knew him would have noticed the way he held the spear, and would have known that from that position, he could loose it at an enemy with a suddenness and force unequaled in the jungle. But, Jules did not take comfort in that fact. His heart was racing and he struggled to quell the fear that threatened to cause him to bolt. He advanced slowly toward the waiting man.  He stopped about twenty feet from the stranger who stood facing him, arms folded and smiling.

Jules said, "I am Jules, hunter of the Wega.  Who are you?"

The stranger smiled and replied, "I am called Cubal by most. Some call me by other names." Cubal picked his cloak from the ground.

"Who are you?"  Jules could feel the presence of this man, the intensity of his being.

Again, the smile. "I have told you who I am. Perhaps you wonder what I am, or where I am from?"

Jules nodded.

"I come from there." Cubal swept his arm upward to the stars. "There, many years from this place, I was born. I came for a time of trouble, and when that time passed, I was in a world which did not need me nor want me. So, I became a traveler."

Cubal smiled again at Jules and continued, "And your world is my third stop." He paused, looked at the jungle where the Bora tiger had disappeared and added, "Your beast welcomed me and thought to have me stay longer than I intend."

At this, Jules laughed. The tension ran from the big man and he said, "You must come to my village as my guest. I would seat you at my table."

Cubal said, "It would do me great honor to sit at your table and to be your  guest." Cubal strode forward and extended his arm, palm forward. Jules backed away and the other laughed and said, "Forgive me. It is my way of greeting."

Jules managed a smile, then said, "Here, we greet one another this way." The big man raised his spear and made a motion as if to throw it at Cubal who remained motionless; but the relaxed, friendly air about the man vanished, and Jules shivered as the other's eyes rested on his. He felt the man's look—actually felt it physically! He felt the presence of death in the stranger, felt the danger radiating from him. Jules shivered again and lowered the spear. Immediately the feeling vanished.

*This is the most dangerous being ever to walk upon my world.* The thought sent a small chill down his spine.

Jules said, "If a man is your friend, he will lower his weapon with you if he has one, and if he does not have a weapon, he will fold his hand upon his chest. The other will do the same."

Jules studied the man closely. He continued, "How did you do that?"

"You mean the feeling that you got when you held your spear raised at me?"

Jules was startled. "Yes! You knew it, then. You did that on purpose. How is such a thing possible?"

The other smiled and said, "My friend, there are many things you do not know about me and many things I will not tell you, but I can tell you that I have been trained for war even from my infancy. It is part of my training that enables me to project my life force."

Jules asked, "Is this the thing that enabled you to send Bora into the jungle?"

Cubal shrugged and replied, "Perhaps. It was a strange creature. I have never before met an animal with as much vitality. The beast shouted at me with its life."

Jules remarked, "You shouted back."

Cubal laughed aloud. "It is a way of putting what happened, yes."

"How could you meet the Bora like that and not be bitten nor scratched? I can understand why the Bora slunk away, for I too have felt your power on my flesh."

6

Cubal paused a long moment, then replied, "My friend, it would take me a lifetime to explain it to you. Be content with this: I met the life force of the Bora and squeezed it until it shrank from me. The physical attack that you saw was not where the real battle was being fought. That was merely a matter of deflecting forces and countering death with life—of providing motion where death demanded stillness."

The lithe man took a deep breath and concluded: "The Bora's life force was the strongest in an animal that I have ever encountered. Any other creature would have embraced death."

Jules asked, "You cannot, then, slay the Bora?"

One corner of Cubal's mouth lifted in that strange little smile he possessed and he said softly, "If it were necessary, I could cause the Bora to release its life force."

Jules pondered the words for a moment, started to ask another question, then shoved the question back from his tongue and said gruffly, "Enough. Come to my home and there you may speak your strange thoughts to men wiser than myself. They may understand you. Jules is but a hunter, not a diviner."

The two men slipped into the jungle quietly. Jules glanced behind him now and then as they went because of the other's uncanny silence. Not a twig cracked, nor was there a whisper of sound as the man followed.

But Jules could feel his presence.

# Chapter 2

*"For every positive force, there is a negative force. If one is to prevail, one must possess greater life force."* D'VRU, BOOK ONE: *The Force of Life*

Cubal was the object of every man, woman and child's attention from the moment he entered the village. Jules stood in a small clearing, clad now in the dark green robe he wore when he was not hunting, and carefully told his story about the Bora tiger. He flushed deeply when he saw the looks of disbelief come to many faces. Exclamations of unbelief echoed in whispers throughout the gathering of people.

There were several snickers, and one voice even suggested that Jules had been sampling the sap of a certain well known tree. It had not occurred to Jules that anyone would doubt him. He was a respected man with his people—a warrior without equal. He glared at the mass of faces and his anger rose to a dangerous level.

"Jules, you have fallen from a tree today. Is that it?" The speaker was a huge man, dressed in dark leather skins, a heavy-boned man known for his strength and for his endurance. His heavy mane of hair was wild, and a dark beard covered a face that, while darkened by the two suns of the planet, was much lighter than the skin of Jules and the people in the village. He stood with teeth showing in a big grin, which belied the roughness in his voice. He held a heavy staff of hardened Ma'tas wood, intricately carved with patterns of beasts, including the Bora tiger, surrounding the staff. Dark stains attested to the use of the staff as a weapon.

Jules' face flushed again, and suddenly, with a shout of anger, he rammed his way through the crowd toward the speaker. Jules slammed his open palms into the larger man's chest, knocking the other backward. The staff fell to the ground. The big man recovered swiftly and before Jules could move, grabbed him and lifted him high above his head. With a mighty surge of muscles and a roar, the man tossed Jules as easily as one might toss a small bundle of rags. Jules tumbled through the air and landed heavily on the grass, nearly thirty feet from the other. He rolled and came to his feet, flooded with a deadly rage. Jules loosed the leather tie to his green cloak, and with a look of eager determination, moved toward his target, his hand close beside the razor-sharp blade at his side. He knew Antal well and understood the man's strength was too much for even three men like himself. Antal's strength was legend.

But no man, save the stranger, was as fast or as deadly a fighter as Jules. He closed in on the giant who stood waiting, unafraid, eager to join in battle with a man who he knew would not be easy to conquer. He did not think Jules was the equal of Antal—not with spear, nor blade, nor strength. Only Jules' speed did he acknowledge. Antal drew his blade and stood silent, waiting.

Suddenly, just as the two men were beginning to circle one another, preparatory to their duel to the death, Cubal stepped between them.

"Let there be peace, my friends. It is not proper that you should fight over this thing. I am shamed that I have brought this quarrel to your village." Cubal held his hand up toward each man.

Jules stopped circling, still wary, his anger still riding him. He said, "I will stop because my friend desires it." He glared at Antal, and with promise in his voice, added, "We shall deal with this matter at another time."

The giant growled and retorted, "We will fight now, Jules. You think to escape me with use of your strange friend. You have begun and now we must finish."

Cubal spoke, his words suddenly strong and commanding. Jules marveled at the force, the impact the man could bring to his voice:

"No! There shall not be battle between yourself and Jules." He stared intently at the man called Antal.

Antal felt that gaze and sensed power radiating from the stranger, a feeling unlike anything he'd ever experienced. He stared back, but the other would not look away. Antal said with a growl, "Perhaps you would prefer to fight for Jules."

The giant grinned and looked around at the crowd, then added, "After all, the slayer of Bora tigers should not fear a battle with a mere man." The crowd laughed.

Jules surged forward, but Cubal placed a hand on the man's chest, and Jules was stopped as though he'd run against a Ma'tas tree which has no bend in it. "No, my friend. I believe perhaps this is the best way, after all. Unless I prove your words, you will have lost much in the eyes of your people."

He turned to Antal and said softly, "I see that you are one possessed of great strength. Perhaps a contest of strength would interest you?"

Antal puzzled over the question, then asked, "A contest of strength with you?" Laughter swept the crowd for it was obvious to all of them that the stranger, although clearly muscular, was no match for the towering Antal.

"I propose a contest between the two of us to decide who is the stronger." Cubal stood before the giant with his arms folded.

Antal growled, "I will carry ten men through the village, little one, and if you should somehow manage to carry five men, I will then carry fifteen men."

Cubal smiled. "I have a better contest. Since you have shown that you are a great thrower of men, let us see who can throw the other the greater distance."

A gasp of amazement burst from the crowd and whispers swept over it. The giant laughed loudly and said, "You would seek to throw Antal?" The crowd laughed with Antal this time.

"Yes. I will let you throw me first. After all, I am a guest, and it is only right that I be tossed first." Cubal extended his arms and stood waiting.

The giant looked for a long moment, then swiftly the man strode over to the waiting Cubal, grabbed the smaller man by a shoulder, reached down, grabbed a thigh and lifted Cubal high over his head. The big man took one step back, arched slightly, and with a sudden flexing of his massive legs and body, gave an deafening roar and hurled Cubal into the air. A shout of approval erupted from the crowd.

The roar stopped as suddenly as it had begun, replaced by startled cries of amazement. The stranger they'd seen flung as a loose sack of rags had curled himself into a ball in mid-flight—a ball that was whirling rapidly—a whirling ball of human flesh which had changed directions and had inexplicably moved toward Antal. The whirling black ball moved just over the giant's head, then suddenly uncurled itself, and the stranger dropped from the air directly behind the giant.

"You have not thrown me very far."

Antal whirled around and stared in disbelief. *It was the wind! The wind had blown the stranger, surely.*

But no, there was no wind. All was still and not a leaf on the nearby Ather tree rustled.

Antal said, "You are one of the devils."

Cubal smiled and said, "No. I am a warrior, trained from before my birth. I simply executed a maneuver known to men such as myself from their childhood."

Cubal moved near the giant, and before the man could protest, he lifted the big man effortlessly from the ground and tossed him. Antal flew nearly ten feet in the air. An audible gasp swept the crowd. Antal hit the ground heavily and rolled. He sat up, put both palms on the ground, and leaned back on his arms, staring at Cubal, his mouth slack with astonishment.

However, it was not the fact that he'd been thrown which so impressed the big man, but the certain knowledge that the stranger could have tossed him much further than that. There had not been the barest of exertion from the stranger. Antal had felt the man's power. It was in his very touch, but something more. Much more.

The giant rose slowly from the ground. He looked at Jules, then back to Cubal. Then, he turned to the crowd. "We have been foolish and Jules has brought us the truth about the stranger." He shifted his gaze to Jules and said, "I am sorry for mocking you, Jules. I was a fool."

The big man turned to Cubal and said, "You would teach Antal these things?"

Cubal laughed. "I can teach Antal many things, but I cannot teach him to throw men."

Antal replied, "Teach Antal how to be thrown as you were thrown, stranger."

"Some things can only be learned as a child, my friend."

"Teach me to be a child, stranger."

Cubal's eyebrows raised. "There is more to you than is apparent, friend." He looked at the crowd and said, "But enough of this. Let us continue getting to know one another. I wish to know all there is to know about you, and I will tell you of myself and my travels."

Long into the night, the village sat around listening as Cubal told them of strange worlds, of strange beasts, and stranger beings. He was a skillful speaker, able to use words as a painter uses a brush to paint his picture. Even the children listened quietly, respectfully, and in complete rapture. And then, the men told Cubal of their world, of their ways, and of the dangers in their world.

Although familiar with some things of their planet, he was ignorant of most of the world. He listened intently as they told him of a world that was, in many places, covered with lush vegetation, a jungle of trees and plants watered by blue clouds which burst with an unpredictable thunder of noise, raining down its contents upon the jungle with daily regularity. But, there were other parts of their world that were stark, empty of vegetation, barren of soil, and received no moisture ever. It was a desolate portion where no life walked.

They told him of the only two cities they knew about, and spoke of the rich mining fields near one of them, but he was surprised to learn that they had never ventured into the cities. No one could tell him why, other than those had been forbidden places as long as anyone could remember. There was danger for them there. They could not tell him of the dangers because they had never been told what they were, but only that they should never go into the cities. Cubal already knew about some of those dangers, because in the main city there was a trading port, and it was infamous for certain things. They were right to stay away from the cities.

The older ones told him of times of wars, though there had been no wars now for dozens of years, and of hunting expeditions that would come into the jungles—strange, off-world beings flown in by strange craft, off-loaded and left there for long spans of time. The craft would return moons later. Caged beasts would be loaded into the craft, as well as some dead beasts. A few of the older men in the village had once seen a Bora tiger loaded, its whiteness darkened on one side by the flash of heat and light they'd seen strike the beast causing it to be still.

Finally, near the early part of the morning, Cubal stood suddenly and said, "Enough.  I have taken too much of your time. You have work to do, and I have a desire to see other parts of your world." He paused, then added, "There are things that I must do in your world."

Jules and the giant Antal stood almost in unison.  Jules said, "Cubal, may I...," he looked quickly at Antal, then continued, "that is, may we accompany you in your journey?"

Cubal said,  "I go to the city. There will be danger there."

Antal and Jules both looked at each other and grinned, and Jules said,  "We must go and see this place with you." Jules did not say it, but he knew that with this man, he'd feel secure no matter what enemy they met there.

"Well then, it is good. I was hoping for another to guide me.  It is even better that I have two guides."

It took little time for the men to prepare for the journey. The two men gathered a few things, and said their goodbyes, while Cubal stood waiting near the edge of a cliff, looking down over the vastness of a jungle below.  In the far distance, he could see what he assumed was the city known by the Ati as Gorgta, but known to Cubal as The City of Scales, so named by a Journeyman Trader many ages ago. It was given this name because of the great emphasis placed on balances by the populace.  In their mind, there was a scale for everything, and nothing existed that could not be weighed and balanced.

Cubal had deliberately avoided entering the city on his arrival, although the space port was there.  He still did not know why he'd not entered there when he'd first arrived.  His intentions had been to land at the space port and spend some time in the city, meeting the people, learning the ways and culture of this world, and following the feelings that had led him to the planet. Instead, when nearing the planet, he suddenly reached over and switched off the receptor for the port beam used to take all vessels into the space port. An hour later, he'd landed on the edge of the jungle near the place where the Bora tiger had stalked him.

Cubal trusted his instincts. What was impulse to another, was survival to him. There was a reason for the diversion. He'd know, eventually. It was enough for him to know that there was danger in that place for him.

Antal walked heavily up to Cubal, his staff in one hand, a spear in the other, a sword buckled around his huge waist, and a small disc shoved into the front of his belt. Cubal reached out, removed the disc, and began examining it.

"Where did you get this?"

Antal grunted, then replied, "A stranger from the city lost it on a trail. I was following him and saw it fall."

Cubal asked, "Do you know its use?"

Antal grinned and said, "Perhaps not, but I have a use for it. I think perhaps I discovered its secret."

Cubal handed him back the disc and said, "Show me your use."

Antal took the disc, looked around him and spied a target, a small boulder several dozen yards distance. Suddenly, he hurled the disc at the target. The power in the big man's throw caused the disc to hum as it sped toward the target. The impact of the disc shattered the boulder, fragmenting it into many small pieces.

The giant walked over to retrieve the disc. Cubal studied him carefully, his face a reflection of thought. The giant had surprised him twice, now. Truly, this man was not what he appeared.

As the big man padded back, disc in hand, Cubal said, "Antal, how is it that you thought to so use the disc?"

The giant thought for a long moment, then replied, "It had no other value to me. If it was a part of some of the city machines, I could not use it. I learned that it was impossible to break. I have tried every way to even scratch it. So, I began throwing it at things. It seems to take the power I give it for flight and use it somehow against the object it strikes."

Cubal's eyebrows raised and he said softly, "Truly, you astound me." He stared at the giant for a long moment, then asked, "Have you always lived here in the jungle, Antal?"

Antal nodded, then said, "I have dreams of another world, but it is not a world I have ever seen except in my dreams. This jungle and these people are all I have ever known, Cubal."

"Who is your mother?"

He pointed down the hill to a solitary woman standing watching them. "She with the pale attire. That is Alish, the Curious. I have no father."

"No father? Did he die?"

Antal shrugged, clearly not liking the conversation. He sighed and said, "My mother will not talk of my father." He turned and walked away, moving down the hill toward Alish.

Jules left a small hut and began moving up the hill to Cubal. As he reached him, Cubal, his eyes on Alish and Antal, said, "Jules, who is the father of Antal?"

Jules flushed, started to answer, then said, "It is forbidden to speak of that matter, Cubal." He stared hard at Cubal and added, "I see that you have powers of perception as well."

Cubal glanced at him, then turned back to gaze at the jungle below. "I do not believe Antal is the son of Alish, and I do not believe he is of the tribe of Anti.

"Truly you have the gift of sight. None but the old ones know this thing and you see it."

Cubal turned to look at Jules. "And how is it that you know?"

Jules replied, "I was with Alish when she found Antal. He was but a child."

"Was he alone?" Now that Cubal had guessed at most of the secret, Jules did not hesitate to tell him the story. He stepped up near Cubal and as they stood gazing down at the jungle and the city, he talked.

"I rode a small pala with Alish. She was older and used to take me for rides. We heard a loud noise and saw a small ship leave the jungle, so we rode over to observe. As we rode up, Alish spied a child, Antal, standing alone beside a post. The post had strange faces on it, and Antal was tied to the post by a long cord. The cord was around his waist and was tied in such a way as to be unremovable."

Jules patted his knife and continued, "We cut the cord and took him to the village. Alish claimed him as her find, and the law stated that she was entitled to the find, though it had never been applied in this manner. Since there was fear of some kind of vengeance or attack against us for loosing the child, a decision was made that he would become one of us, and so, it became a secret shared only by the older ones and Alish and myself."

"Antal does not know?"

"No. He suspects, but he does not know."

Cubal smiled and said, "He may surprise you and himself, one day."

With that, he moved down the hill toward the giant figure moving their way. Jules gathered his belongings and followed.

In the days that followed, the trio made its way through the jungles, up steep mountains and across many rivers. Cubal was convinced that Antal was a member of the ancient M'naros culture from the planet Ex'tal. He remembered the stories he'd been told during his training as a warrior.

Part of his training was to learn the ways of virtually every creature known to the Council of Worlds. This race had been of particular interest to Cubal because its people seemed to him to have powers that were not ordinary. They could do things with their mind, such as move objects, and they often, though not always, possessed some of the mental skills naturally that Cubal had developed as a warrior. The one time Cubal had visited the planet to assist in fighting against a particularly vicious enemy, he'd met men who were fierce warriors, who had the shifting power.

It explained the times when Cubal had not noticed Antal's movements. It was as though there had been a lapse in time for Cubal. Suddenly, the man had appeared beside him, and Cubal had not known he was coming, nor did he comprehend how he got there. It had been unsettling for Cubal, whose senses were not used to being deceived. Antal had the power of dimensional shifting, the same power he'd seen the warriors on Ex'tal use.

Cubal spent many hours in that journey teaching Antal many things and probing for the secret of his ability to shift his being from one location to another instantly. He made Antal tell him in detail the exact sequence of his thoughts, and even insisted on a detailed explanation of exactly how he felt just before the shift. Antal knew the secret, but it was difficult in getting him to share it for it was something the giant did without conscious thought. He did not know how he did what he did. He just knew he could do it. Getting him to sequence his thoughts had been difficult.

Then, one day while standing beside a river, Cubal understood. It was in the power of the mind to control the body, but it was also a matter involving the will, and was a matter of bringing the mind to a certain focus. It had to do with moving the mind into a different level, and then willing the body to follow.

Standing beside the river, Cubal called Antal: "Come here, friend."

The big man came near and stood silently before Cubal. "What is it?" he asked.

"I have your secret."

The big man's eyes widened and he smiled. "How is that so? No one has ever understood such a mystery. Even I do not understand it."

Cubal said softly, "Watch." And with that, he disappeared. A shout from across the river, nearly fifty yards distant brought their attention around immediately. Cubal was standing there, arm raised, smiling.

*He had a new weapon now.*

# Chapter 3

*"The senses are an extension of the life force. To control the senses, one must control the life force." D'VRU, BOOK ONE: The Force of Life*

The smell of the city was nearly overpowering. The human odor mingled with alien forms and with the refuse the inhabitants casually dropped into the streets refuse that was intermittently devoured by wild, dog-like creatures and other beasts that roamed the streets freely. The glistening white of the Tathian police helmets were in stark contrast to the dull ugliness of the streets and the somber, black brick buildings. Vendors broadcast imagery scenes into the street causing the uninitiated to veer aside in an attempt to avoid collisions with machines, weapons, jewels, and hordes of other goods. Cubal walked through the illusions, blocking them from his senses, focusing instead on the life forces about him which were vibrant and strong.

He felt the gaze of several of the policemen, then quickly, the feeling passed. He sensed other looks more sinister and spotted three large aliens standing near what Cubal recognized as a small space corridor. Such devices usually led to a waiting ship above, or a permanent planet-fall site. An innocent walking too near would be tossed into the corridor and would wake up on a spacer bound for the Luga mining camps, or worse, the Pegos jungles, digging for the green clay craved by a universe. It was said to enhance one's life, to give one wisdom and health. Cubal suspected it was merely another of the universe's illusions.

Cubal did not deviate from his path. He saw the smug, knowing look of a nearby policeman as he passed. The policeman's burly form melded into the shadows of a building. He would not be interfering. Probably, he was paid not to interfere.

Antal padded quietly along beside Cubal, with Jules following a few paces behind them. As they neared the three aliens, Cubal said softly, "Antal, move away from me. Jules, stay back."

The big man did not miss a step as he veered away. Cubal could feel the big man's awareness quicken and his life force radiate. He marveled. Antal's life force was vibrant and strong, more than most he'd ever touched. Cubal continued walking.

The aliens appeared to be from one of the newer planets which entered into the Trading Federation. They were big, humanoid, with a pale, luminous skin, and their dark green eyes were unusually large. Their hands were splayed with three talon-like fingers and a thumb that resembled a human thumb, only much larger. Each wore a thin, loose-fitting grey-colored garment, and a cloak of the same color.

Suddenly, one of the aliens leaped behind Cubal and reached out in order to propel him into the corridor. The alien gasped as his own momentum was suddenly redirected by unseen hands, and instantly, he was propelled forward with a speed that defied his best abilities to stop his momentum. In a mere second of time, the alien disappeared within a shimmer of pale green light as his body hurtled through the space corridor. Cubal knew he would be falling into a dark green jungle or a waiting slave ship.

The alien nearest Cubal snorted in surprise, its slitted green eyes widening and his slender lipless mouth forming a perfect circle. The alien began a slow, weaving walk toward Cubal. It was the walk of one trained as a Caleh fighter, a combination of philosophies whose methods included use of the deadly Mer gas and explosive powders.

Cubal stood waiting, completely relaxed. He sensed Antal moving forward, so he held his hand up and said softly, "Stay, friend. This one is dangerous, and his companion is even more dangerous. You would die here if you advance. Stay out of the fight."

Cubal moved slowly to one side, moving away from Antal. Jules stood silently, spear held in that peculiar tilt, ready to hurl it, but watching. He had seen what Antal had not, and what the two strange beings had not witnesed He had seen the battle with the deadly Bora tiger. This warrior would not need Jules' help this night. And, if these two had seen what he'd seen with the tiger, they'd be backing away, not moving to the attack.

Cubal knew the two would work as a team. The one continued his slow weaving walk toward him while the other moved in from the opposite direction, advancing on Cubal from the side, his hands hidden in the folds of his supple, dark cape.

Suddenly, the air filled with a strange fragrance. The alien approaching Cubal from the front had leaped backward, and now stood watching Cubal intently, his narrow, lipless mouth formed into an evil grin of expectancy. Suddenly, the grin dissolved as disbelief washed over the creature's face. He stared incredulously as the stranger stood facing him, arms folded across his chest, his lips holding the suggestion of a smile. The man should be asleep on the ground by now from the knockout gas he'd released, but the stranger showed no signs of being affected.

The alien leaped forward with a shout of rage, and his companion also rushed forward, his hands flashing from beneath his robes in a blur of motion. The air began emitting sparks and showers of lightening as the aliens tossed small explosive globlets at the dark-cloaked man. But, Cubal was not there. He'd begun his movements a fraction of a second before they'd made their moves. By the time they'd tossed their explosives, Cubal was already in the air, leaping over their heads. He landed behind them, nearly twenty feet away from the aliens.

Cubal moved toward the nearest creature, his hands circling, feeling the life force, testing it, focusing on it. The alien waited, unsure of whether to run or fight. He saw his companion standing to one side and knew the other was waiting to see the outcome. He wished he could be an observer, too, but it was too late for that, now.

*I must escape this strange human.*

With a speed that belied his huge bulk, the alien whirled around and leaped in the opposite direction, but his momentum was suddenly enhanced by an unseen hand and his direction was slightly diverted. All of his energies at escaping were now being directed and controlled. He felt the pressure, but could not see the hand that propelled him forward. He could not change his course. The corridor flickered with that strange, pale green glow, then swallowed him as it had his companion earlier. A crackle of noise sounded and he winked out of sight.

The remaining alien began backing away, fear now completely controlling him. He'd witnessed something he still could not understand. He'd heard of strange warriors such as this one, deadly without appearing to be, walking as humans, but taking life as a god.

*The tales were true. This was one!* He now knew that the stories about strange men who dressed in black robes and left death in their wake were not the fables he'd assumed.

A sharp prick at his back stopped his backward movement. He'd noticed the strange native with the spear standing in the shadows and knew this was the one now at his back. A quiet voice said, "Do not move or I will bring death." The voice was spoken matter-of-fact without emotion.

Cubal moved to the alien and stood before him, that strange little smile on his face. He said, "Good work, Jules." He stepped closer and said to the alien, "If you move your hands, especially the one clutching the Mer capsule, I will end your life force instantly. I can remove the life that is within you before you can hurl your gas, and if your feet move, you will be dead before your head lands on the ground." He paused and gazed at the other intently.

Jules knew Cubal was doing that strange thing with the mind that he'd done in the jungle with Jules, as well as speaking in that different voice, a commanding, powerful voice. He knew a little of what the alien was probably feeling.

The alien grunted as he felt the impact of the other's look and as the power of the man's voice penetrated his mind. Fear flooded his being. There was nothing hid from the stranger. His fingers relaxed their grip on the gas capsule. The rope-like tendons in his feet spread out in a relaxed stance.

Cubal said, "You have two choices." He nodded at the corridor, then said, "There, or there." He pointed to the ground. "I can leave you on the ground with your life force crushed and gone."

The alien looked at the ground as comprehension set in. His mind raced to the image of the jungle slave force. He'd never seen them, but he'd heard it described from a few who'd delivered slaves in the old days by ship. Strange beings took slaves and worked them deep in the jungles digging for the green clay. No one ever returned from the jungles.

The mining colony was a far better fate. Escape from there was common, and it was possible to bribe one's way out. He swallowed hard. He did not know where the corridor was set this day. It had been set for the jungles a midnight ago. He did not have the responsibility of keying in the receptor. He never really cared where it went—not until now. He looked around quickly, hoping for some way of escape. Against the two men who stood with the strange warrior, the alien would have attempted to fight free, but not against the stranger. Death—his own—would be certain. He knew that. He glanced over at the silent, watchful policeman. The policeman made no move to interfere.

With a low growl, the alien nodded at the corridor and stepped forward. In another second he was at the entrance. He stepped to the edge, and as he did, he knew that he would have his vengeance, if not his freedom. He stepped into the pale green light of the corridor and simultaneously flicked the deadly gas capsule at the black clad stranger.

But, as quickly as he had flicked the gas capsule, Cubal was even quicker. Even before the capsule left the alien's hands, Cubal was moving. He'd seen the slight movements of the shoulders, had seen the look in the creature's eyes, and as the capsule moved from the alien's gnarled hand, even as it began emitting its deadly gases, Cubal leaped forward, and with a flicker of a finger, knocked the capsule into the corridor with the disappearing alien. Both the capsule and the alien disappeared into darkness.

Cubal moved away from the corridor, his mind and body focused intently on driving out the gases from his pores. Although he'd knocked the capsule back, a small amount had reached his skin and was attempting to penetrate. His mind locked onto those particular pores, and suddenly he felt them work together to propel the gas molecules outward and away. He stepped back and relaxed.

Jules said, "The little pebble is danger to you?" It was more a statement than a question.

Cubal smiled. "It is deadly, my friend. One small brush with Mer gas and your life force will dissolve."

"Why did you not die, then? I saw the yellow touch your skin on the hand."

Cubal's eyes widened with surprise. "You vision is very good to have seen the gas. Few can. I sensed the entry points of the Mer gas and closed those entrances after expelling the gas."

Antal said, "Can you close all of your skin to such a thing?"

Cubal raised his eyebrows at the giant. "Yes, but not for very long. To deny the body breath through the skin will raise the temperature within and cause eventual death."

"Will you teach me this?"

Cubal smiled. "I do not think this is a thing that can be learned by one of your age, friend. It is a thing taught to a child and practiced as the child grows. Indeed, not everyone who knows of the technique can master it." Some who'd trained with him were unable to selectively close pores in their skin after a life-time of effort. It had taken him seventeen years to master it.

# Chapter 4

*"The measure of force that one extends toward another is both strength and weakness. Vulnerability may lie in that extension." D'VRU, BOOK ONE: The Force of Life (Strengths and Weaknesses)*

The trio slipped into the dense crowd, melting into the myriad of strange faces and shapes. Man-like creatures dominated, outnumbering those whose appearance was so strikingly dissimilar that one knew instantly that its origins were non-human, that no human lineage would ever be found in such beings. Some were clearly reptilian, with a disposition to match their repulsiveness. Others were merely different, strange beings from strange worlds, all living or visiting on the planet Na'ha, or as called in the Mecadorian tongue, *Lag'hangu te ra'sna*. Humans had long ago reduced the name to a more pronounceable sound, and it had stuck, and, excepting for some of the aged inhabitants of the planet, it was Na'ha to all.

Na'ha was a trading planet. It hung central to the Meridos system, had a radiant gravity that was acceptable to all but the largest of species, and its atmosphere was rich in oxygen and several gases that, while not harmful to humans, was essential to some of the other alien forms of life. It was this gas mixture that made the planet attractive as a trading planet.

It also attracted the evil of the galaxy for it was a place to find slaves, a place to trade slaves—a place to buy and sell anything in the universe, including weapons of virtually any kind and description. The law on Na'ha was a simple one, written by the Neimic government thousands of years ago and maintained by those who'd come after them. The law, roughly translated, said: "Unseat not the government by force, but by natural causes it shall abate, and the citizens shall be free to do as they please. A force shall police the land for the good of the government and the good of the land in a manner that shall be approved by the government."

There were no other written laws in Na'ha, though there were thousands of unwritten policies and rules that carried the force of law. The police permitted the slavers to operate their portals, only restricting them in the number of slaves they could take in a day, exempting certain classes of citizens, including government officials, and requiring them to post their portals only at selected places in the city.

It was a way for the government to control the massive population explosion that had come with the planet's popularity as a trading center. The regular inhabitants of the city knew where the portals were and stayed far from them. But now and then, the slavers would send out bands of kidnappers, and they often set up illegal portals in the jungles where they would bring those they'd captured, including various animals used for rich hunters. It was one of the most profitable businesses in the universe.

"Cubal. What is that strange sound?" Antal had stopped and was listening intently.

Jules stopped beside him. "What sound? I hear nothing but the strange grunts and squeaks of this crowd, and that sound has been with us since we set foot in this city. Everywhere, there are strange sounds, and you speak of a strange sound? " Jules' eyebrows were raised with curiosity as he stared at his friend.

Cubal turned to Antal, a look of genuine surprise on his face. "You can hear the Putsha?"

Antal replied, "Putsha I do not know. But there are strange words and sounds in my head, and I do not like it. Also, I see movement in the shadows that appear to be with the sounds."

Cubal smiled. He looked at Jules and said, "Antal is far more than he appears, my friend. Far more. There are few who can detect the voice of the Putsha."

"And who are these Putsha? Where are they?" Antal's head whirled around, his deep green eyes searching the crowd intently.

Cubal said softly, "Putsha are hidden in the corners and crevices of some cities. They are a small, caniverous animal, vaporous in appearance, and thus they remain hidden from all but the eyes of those who know how to see them. They sing to each other during the day, and in the night, they hunt."

"Hunt? What do they hunt?" Jules was now curious.

Cubal smiled. "They hunt food, even as a jungle beast hunts for food." He paused, stretched his hand out, swept it around, and added, "This is their jungle." Cubal paused again and with a sweep of his hand continued, "And all flesh are prey for the Putsha."

Consternation swept over the faces of the two. "You mean we are going to be stalked by creatures too small for us to see and we may become their supper?" Antal was becoming concerned.

"It is true that they would view you as a choice meal. Your size would keep them filled for many months. But, it is not likely they will find you tonight, and even if they did, it would take too many of them to bring you down because you hear them. If one can hear the Putsha, one can see the Putsha. You would see them, and therefore they will look for easier prey. You are in no danger, friend."

"What about me? Am I prey for them?"

Cubal smiled at his nervous friend. "No, Jules. As long as you are with me or as long as you are in a safe dwelling during the night hours, you will not be prey for the Putsha."

Jules thought on this for a long moment, then asked, "And this place of safety, what is this place?"

"It is a structure that has filters which echo any Putsha voices that enter, and then makes them vulnerable. They have learned to avoid such places. Thus, it is the ignorant who walk the streets at night, or who seek shelter in dwellings that are unfiltered, who are most at risk. We will seek a dwelling that is filtered, though not for your sake. I am searching for someone, and he will be in such a place because he knows of the Putsha and would probably have to rely upon a safe dwelling."

With that, Cubal fell silent and the trio moved forward again. Now and then, Antal would shake his head as if to dislodge the strange sounds in his head. Clearly, the giant was not completely pleased with his ability to hear the Putsha.

The second sun was dimming when Cubal led them into a large, green and white structure. As they entered, Antal exclaimed, "They're gone! It is good to be here." He was smiling.

"The filters take the noises from outside away. It is only when the Putsha come into the perimeter of the filter zone that their sounds are amplified, and they will become visible to all. They stay far from such places. For them, to be seen is to die." He stepped upon a slow rising lip of polished amber and it gently lifted him up toward the upper reaches of the structure.

Antal watched then followed, stepping on another lip. Jules managed to step quickly on the same lip, nervous, not liking his surroundings at all. As they rose, his eyes were in constant motion as he glanced at everything quickly, evaluating it all for danger, too uneasy to appreciate the wonder of it all, or the beauty of some of it.

There were many different beings sitting around talking or walking to some unknown destination for unknown business, sometimes alone, sometimes in groups or pairs. Everywhere, there was movement, and everywhere, there were idle, lounging individuals. Antal felt himself relaxing. There did not seem to be a sense of the danger he had while in the street.

Cubal directed them to a small enclave where there were huge lounges. "Wait here until I return. Do not accept any invitations to go anywhere. Do not accept anything. No drinks. No food."

He disappeared around a corner and the two men settled gently into the soft embrace of the lounges. Antal glanced at Jules and said, "I would sleep if you will watch." He knew Jules would be too nervous to sleep. Jules nodded, his eyes flickering around as he gladly took on the role of guardian.

Several levels above them, Cubal was entering a huge room. There were uniformed aliens in the room at one corner. In the center of the room, covering a huge section of the flooring was a large, circular plate of polished diamond. Directly above, in the ceiling, was a large telescope-like mechanism. Encircling the plate was a radiant, supple ribbon of polished light-berl, the hardest, most pliable material in the known universe. It's touch would burn, and it was often used as a corral for animals on many worlds. Sometimes, it was used to beat prisoners. Five lashes of light-berl were akin to a dozen lashes with a whip made of the Kylanian lizard, whose scales rip and tear at one's flesh.

Cubal moved closer, watching curiously as a small band of A'rkji, flesh-eating man hunters he'd come to despise on Kroys'nan, began removing a prisoner from a cage. His eyes swept the group quickly, then focused on the uniformed soldiers. He knew the man he was looking for was not here. The black-clad warrior began moving back slowly, blending himself into the crowd. He had long ago learned the art of blending, of making his life force diminish so as not to alert those who might seek him as prey or sense him as competition. It was not that he feared anyone in the room. But, he still had that sense of danger, that sense that told him someone or something waited here for him, probably to harm him. Therefore, it would be wise for him to be as the Putsha, invisible to his unknown enemies.

Suddenly, as he was moving toward the outer edges of the room, he heard the prisoner of the A'rkji cry out. He stopped suddenly.

*I know that voice!*

He knew the identity of the prisoner of the A'rkji. And, he also knew that his desire to remain invisible was now going to be impossible. Cubal knew the ones he sought was in this array of buildings somewhere. That person or group would surely know of his presence in just a few seconds. Those who sought him would now be alerted when he acted to rescue the prisoner.

He moved with the quick glide of a big cat moving swiftly across an open field to take down its prey. Cubal kept the extension of his life force at a level that would not be noticeable to the A'rkji. He saw them hurl the prisoner onto the diamond plate. The man slid across the polished surface on his back, spinning around until he came to rest in the center. He again cried out in pain, and Cubal saw streaks of blood across his stomach. He'd been beaten, probably with a Kylanian whip. It was a favorite of the A'rkji.

Cubal moved near the A'rkji and watched as one of them began punching at a pad controlling the mechanism in the ceiling. He knew that if he did not move quickly, his friend would be instantly transported, probably to the home of the A'rkji, for food. This was only the second interstellar transporter of this kind he'd ever seen. They were very expensive and their use prohibited on most other worlds. While the ordinary portals could move a person into another world, it did it with the use of an extensive array of jump sites, usually located in ships. Although the leap through a portal would seem instantaneous to the one moving through it, in actuality, the person was moving through several, sometimes dozens, of linked portals.

These were different. They moved through time and space itself. It was said that if the right settings were made, one could move forward or backward in time. Cubal did not know. He did know that this device would transport his friend instantly to the world of the A'rkji, and that his end would be as the main course in a frenzied feeding by some of the elite on that world.

He leaped over the light-bezel and grabbed his friend from the floor. But, he'd barely begun to lift him when the brilliance of a thousand suns swept through his body, and in a millisecond of thought, he knew that the A'rkji would not have a one-course meal, but would have two coming for dinner. In the next second, he was there, standing on a plate of polished diamond. But, little else was the same. Instead, he was in a room filled with A'rkji warriors, each armed with their deadly light guns.

His friend groaned softly as Cubal lifted him from the floor. His mind was calculating the odds. A Wearer of the Black did not fear an enemy and did not fear death. It was never about death for such a one. It was about life force and protecting it, and about measuring the life force of an enemy and determining its vulnerabilities, its weaknesses, and its strengths. Now, it was about protecting two life forces: his and his friend's. He knew that the time was not right. His friend would die if he chose to resist. He slowly lowered his energy level and shrank inside his dark cloak.

Three warriors came up to them, one chortling, "It is good. Two there are for the feeding. It is reward." Roughly, they seized both men and dragged them off the diamond plate, then shoved them down a long, unlit, narrow hall. The dampness of the whole place carried foul odors. After a few moments, the two were propelled into a large room. It was a room of almost complete darkness. Cubal knew that the A'rkji preferred the dark and always fed in the night hours. He could not tell whether it was nightfall or not. But, perhaps they did not need light. Perhaps they only needed the dark.

Cubal closed his eyes for several long seconds, slowed his breathing, then slowly opened his eyes, compelling his vision to adjust for the darkness by absorbing every bit of light possible. It was a technique mastered by every studeny of D'vru. He counted fifteen A'rkji seated at a long trough nearby. He'd heard of the feeding trough but had never seen one. The victim was first disabled by slashing the tendons of the ankles, then thrown into the trough, bleeding. He was then propelled down the trough, each A'rkji at the table slicing a portion from the victim, feeding, then immediately shoving the victim on down to the next A'rkji. It was said that some victims had lived to be passed up the third time. Apparently, it was sport to take only so much, and to keep the victim alive as long as possible. As the memories of the practices of the A'rkji passed through his mind, Cubal smiled. He felt the warrior blood in him rise and felt old, familiar feelings flood his being.

*These beasts will prey no more on human flesh.*

The thought was a manifesto, and he knew that if he had to decimate the entire planet, these beings would not stalk him or his kind again. He set his mind and felt his body moving into the old familiar patterns, feeling the energies there. His hearing became acute and his breathing slowed. Awareness flooded his being.

Suddenly, he stepped away from his guard and moved into the open space. The guard raised his weapon to fire, but one seated at the table raised his hand and in a raspy, hissing voice in the tongue of the A'rkji, said, "Let him speak. It will be added pleasure to the night." The reptilian being smiled, his razor teeth showing even in the dark room.

Cubal's voice was not loud, but it rang with authority. He spoke in the language of the A'rkji, though without the rasp, and hissing certain sounds to form his words as did the A'rkji: "I am Cubal, Wearer of the Black. I have come to bring an end to your life force and to end the existence of all of your kind."

He continued, his voice cutting through the surprised shouts of anger. "You thought to feed on me and my friend. But, I shall take your life force and feed it to the darkness." His last words were spoken almost in a whisper—guttural, and full of promise.

With that, he shrank low to the surface, then whiled around in a complete circle once, fixing the images in his mind of the entire room. His hands moved in the darkness, feeling the forces, feeling their energy and shapes, as he also absorbed the movements in the room with his senses. He moved quickly toward one soldier who, too late, sought to fire his weapon. None saw the death blow rendered to the soldier, nor the ones delivered in silence to the two standing nearby. In barely two seconds of time, three A'rkji warriors lay on the cold floor.

Cubal tossed them casually into the trough and said, "Feed well, A'rkji."

He pushed his friend into a corner and said in a quiet whisper, "Remain here until I come for you."

Those at the feeding trough moved fearlessly toward Cubal, weapons now drawn. Three fired almost in unison, then gasped with astonishment when their target seemed to vanish before their eyes, only to appear beside them. And then, they knew no more of life.

Cubal moved amongst the remaining A'rkji like a cold breath of winter, his presence felt only for a small flicker of time. His movements were not those of an ordinary man, but were as a sudden shift of darkness, which brought instant death. The enemy felt the rage of Cubal penetrate their minds, and fear flood their beings. None of them had ever met such an enemy. Anger at those who'd sent this demon of death to them surged in the leader, the one who'd stayed the hand of the soldier and permitted Cubal to speak.

The A'rkji leader leaped backward, sensing the death coming to him, feeling its closeness, and acutely aware of his inability to stop this darkness from claiming him as its next victim. He landed on the trough, his curved feet gripping the round edges of the wood. As he landed, he said, "Why have you come to slay us? What brings you to our world? You may leave with your friend." The words came in a gush of raspy hisses.

Cubal stopped the death blow already begun at the only survivor. "I came seeking nothing. Your actions have brought me here."

"I do not wish your death, dark warrior. We have heard of such as yourself. You have our peace. I command peace be with you."

Cubal advanced slowly and stopped. "Come forward." His words were powerful, delivered with the techniques of voice command he'd learned and perfected in his training as a warrior.

The creature stepped closer hesitantly, his claws held to his side, and the reptilian head bowed in a servile position. Cubal spoke: "I will honor your word. You say I have your peace. Is yours the word of trust or betrayal?" The hissed words were guttural and broken into the choppy, hissing sounds of the A'rkji tongue, It was a language Cubal had learned many years ago—one which he'd never liked.

The creature responded: "I am Cri, King of all A'rkji, and my word is honor. You have the peace of all A'rkji."

Cubal peered at him intently. His voice rose to a level of command, echoing within the dark walls. "You have your life, Cri, King of A'rkji. But, I give you a warning: Henceforth, A'rkji who seek the death of Cubal or friends of Cubal, will have their life force taken. If you continue to prey on my friends and those who are as I am, then I shall return to your world to destroy you and all who follow you. I will end your existence. There will be no A'rkji life force remaining on the world called A'rkji. This is my promise to you."

The A'rkji king's narrow, grey-green face was one clouded with fear. He'd never met an enemy such as this human. He'd heard of those distant, strange warriors, humans who wore black cloaks, and who were dropped into worlds alone—humans who had destroyed entire armies on those planets. They were legends that some swore were true, while others swore were fables. He knew this was no fable in the room tonight. He'd met the deadliest foe he'd ever faced. The A'rkji would seek peace with such a warrior. To do otherwise was to die. He knew that it would not have mattered that there were a hundred more of his soldiers in the room. They'd have all died at the hands of this strange warrior in black, and who seemed more at home in the darkness of his world than himself.

He stepped forward hesitantly and said, "I will order the death of any A'rkji who seeks the life of Cubal or his friends. You have our peace hereafter. It shall be published here and on all worlds wherein we habit."

Cubal studied the being for a long moment, then added, "Why have you not asked of the identity of the friends of Cubal?"

The lithe creature smiled, its razor teeth gleaming in the small light. "It was assumed by me, great warrior, that Cubal would tell Cri of those names."

Cubal did not return the smile. "My friends are all mankind. They walk as I walk and appear in the form of a human, both male and female, though they may have different skins and features and shapes. They are all human and thus, they are my friends." He paused for a long moment, then, hissing his words, he added: "Do you understand?"

The face of Cri was one of deep consternation for he knew what Cubal meant. Humans had long been a favorite prey for the A'rkji. They usually fought exceptionally well, and they lasted, many of them, longer than other species. To give up such delights was not to his liking and would cause much displeasure within his world. But, Cri was not king for his stupidity.

"You demand a thing that will bring anger and resistance from many in my world. Some will seek my place. "A favor I ask of you in return, Warrior." The creature bowed its head.

"What favor is that?"

Cri said, "It is, no doubt, your pleasure to return to Na'ha. In order to convey a message to my people which will be understood, I must show them why they must accept peace with the Wearer of the Black. If I cannot do this, there are some who may disregard my edict. But, if I can show to those who would doubt me, a display of your powers, then they will accept my declaration of peace with your kind. We will have peace."

"You would sacrifice your officers at Na'ha, those who whipped my friend and sent us here?"

Cri nodded. "It is better than the destruction of us all."

Cubal replied. "I will not return seeking their life force. However, I will return there, and if they seek harm to me or my friend, then I shall indeed show them and you, and whomever you choose to see, the ways of a Wearer of the Black."

Cri nodded and said, "I will send with you a Recorder who shall prepare a Record for me to present to the people. Would you permit that?"

Cubal shrugged. "I care not, Cri, who you send, so long as they seek not my life nor the life of my friend."

Cri smiled. "I promise you, he shall remain silent. He will not provoke, nor intervene, nor even speak."

Cubal nodded his approval, then said, "You will remain away from the controls. I will review them and set them for the journey back."

Cri replied, "There are only 5 settings allowed. The return to Na'ha is expressed with the name of that place, which you will see in the small window on the front."

"I have seen the controls of these devices and understand how they operate. They have a delay mechanism which will allow us to move onto the sending plate." Cubal paused, then continued, his words measured and commanding, "If you move at all during the delay, I will destroy all life on this planet, beginning with yourself. I can be at your side long before you reach the controls.

*This one reads minds!* The slitted eyes of the reptilian creature widened in surprise. It was exactly what he'd planned. He had prepared himself to leap to the panel and press a destination button that would intantly transport Cubal, his companion, and the Recorder, to a planet that was used by the A'rkji solely for the dumping of all of the bones, debri, and other garbage from the planet.

Later, standing on the polished plate, Cubal watched as a small A'rkji walked up to the plate. Cri called to the young A'rkji. "You will stand back and observe everything, especially this one. Do not take your eyes off him. And, you will not interfere. You will not speak. When this man leaves the Halls of K'bla, you will return here."

The young A'rkji nodded, his narrow black eyes darting at Cubal, curiosity in them. *Who was this human who could walk amongst us without death overtaking him? Were the stories of the death of the ruling council true?* His gaze fell away and he stared back at his king.

The king glared at him and said, "Wonder not, Liet. My peace is with this one called Cubal. He is friend to the king and to A'rkji ever after, and all his kind." He stared for a long moment at the black clad warrior, knowing that the instant he was back on Na'ha, the soldiers there would attempt to stop him. And, he knew they'd be helpless before this strange human.

The return was as startling to the senses of Cubal as the original journey had been. He did not like the feeling of disorientation it gave him. At all times, he was in total control of his being, but not for the brief seconds of transport by this machine. It was a discomforting feeling. He did not like the absence of control.

His appearance was sudden and one of surprise to everyone in the room. It was especially surprising to the seven A'rkji soldiers who were stationed there. Two stood near the entry point, and one of them spoke quietly to another. Their hands moved toward their weapons.

"I do not wish to war with you, but I will destroy your life force if you touch your weapons." Cubal spoke in the A'rkji tongue and his voice was harsh, and threatening.

It did not stop them. The Recorder watched, and the scene embedded itself in the visual memory recorder implanted in his head. His eyes darted quickly to the advancing soldiers, then he remembered his king's command to focus on the strange one. He stepped back, moving away from the human and the advancing soldiers, watching intently as the human suddenly leaped at the soldiers. Before they could move, the strange one had struck both soldiers.

The Recorder did not see the blows, but saw the two slump down, and then the remaining five soldiers moved into defensive positions, weapons leveled, seeking to target this human clad in black. Almost instantly, they all died. The Recorder did not see how they died. He just saw them fall back, one gasping, clutching at his neck, another falling clutching his stomach, and the others just falling without sound. In seconds, all five A'rkji warriors lay dead. Cubal slid the first two bodies into the center of the transport plate, then, reached down, and one by one, tossed the other five onto the diamond plate. The Recorder marveled at the ease with which the man tossed the bodies.

"Tell your king to honor the peace and do no harm to humans, or I will return, and there will be no more A'rkji." With that, the strange one turned and left the room. The Recorder looked for a long moment at the dead bodies, then scanned the room, looking at the silent crowd who stood staring at him and the bodies. Then his fingers flickered the pattern necessary for transport and within seconds, he and the bodies disappeared.

The large room was silent for a long moment, then whispers began. Most of those who'd witnessed the event still did not comprehend what they'd seen. But, some did.

One man stood near the back of the room with three others. He said softly, "He is here. We must reach Ka'tre immediately." He moved slowly away from the others to a small cubicle. Once inside, the wall flowed to life, and within seconds, an image flickered onto the wall.

"What news?"

"He is here, Ka'tre. He just stepped off the A'rkji portal and killed the soldiers who man the station."

"Where did he go?"

"I do not know. I have directed Mla to follow with Fl'er."

Ka'tre grimaced. "Fool. He will detect them. You should have directed watchers to station themselves outside. We can locate him there, but if he leaves, we must know where he travels."

"I will set watchers."

Ka'tre waved his hand. "No. I will do it. Just continue to watch there. Do not get close to him. Do not stare at him. Otherwise, you will alert him to yourself."

The tall, thin man-like creature stepped away from the screen and stood for a long minute in deep thought. *He was here. Just as had been prophesied.*

And he, Ka'tre of L'trel, would be the one to capture this destroyer of life, this weapon of destruction. His thin lips parted as he permitted himself a brief moment of pleasure at the thought. He would be a rich man. A very rich man, for the Ancient Ones did not haggle over prices. They were beyond such endeavors. Whatever price was asked for a thing, they paid, and if they did not like the price, they simply looked elsewhere. But they never bargained.

And the price for Cubal, The Wearer of the Black, had been one hundred million Kasels, equal to the entire wealth of the planet, plus one Eeifil Transport superior to the one owned by the A'rkji. Even better, they'd even given him detailed instructions on how to trap the warrior.

But, they'd also warned him. If he failed, there would be severe consequences. If the Wearer of the Black did not find him and destroy him, they would.

He would not fail.

*I will trap this dark warrior for the Ancient Ones.*

# Chapter 5

*"One who measures his strength in terms of his opponent's strength diminishes his life force by a magnitude of seven-fold." D'VRU, BOOK ONE: The Force of Life*

Cubal sat lotus-like on a small mat in the little hut on the outer fringes of the city. Jules stood silent to one side, and Antal squatted to the left of Jules. A lithe young man lay face up in the dirt before them. It was the face of a young man whose skin had been darkened by the shimmering moons of Glale, for his skin had that luminous glow, almost golden in color.

"So, this friend, comes he from Glale?" asked Antal.

Cubal's eyebrows raised. "You know of this place?"

Antal smiled. "Yes. We learned of it from the old ones who told us that strangers once came to visit our village who had skins of gold and wore costumes that glittered of a brilliant blue. They rode devices that appeared to be glowing logs."

Cubal nodded slowly. "Yes, that would be the Glalians. They would be the investigators, those of the blue. They were making inquiries for some reason."

Jules volunteered, "They did not tell us what they were seeking, but after a time, we saw them place an object into one of the logs and they vanished."

Cubal's eyes narrowed and he said, "You said 'we,' Jules. Do you mean you saw this?"

Jules smiled and said, "Of course."

"What is your age, Jules?"

Jules stared for a long minute and then replied, "I do not understand."

"How long have you lived?"

Jules widened his smile. "Yes, I understand. We measure our lives by the red days. I am fifteen red days."

Cubal was surprised. He knew that would make the warrior at least one hundred years old, according to human standards. The man did not look to be over thirty human years.

He looked at Antal and said, "Jules, how long has he lived?"

"I do not know. When he came, he was small. Now he is a giant and twelve red days have come and gone in his time."

Cubal looked back at his friend lying still on the ground inside the small abandoned hut they'd found. Cubal had prepared a potion and given it to him, and now the young man slept the deep sleep of healing. In the morning, he'd awake and soon be restored.

The three talked late into the night, with Jules clearly nervous about not being able to hear or see the Putsha. Cubal assured him that if they came, he and Antal would hear them, and they did not hunt where they were heard. Outside, they heard the sounds of the nearby jungle. Soon, all were asleep except Cubal, who had placed his body and mind into a state of rest which permitted his senses to remain completely alert while his body rested. He was not weary. Nothing he'd done as yet had come close to tiring him.

Warriors like himself, those who wore the robe of Black, had been trained from birth to develop their stamina to remarkable levels. The control of a warrior's mind and body was the first requirement. A warrior had to survive in cold that would kill most life, endure heat that would blister the lungs of humans, and live without food or water for periods of time impossible for ordinary men.

On this night, he rested quietly, contemplating his future. He was being hunted, that much he knew, and his curiosity had driven him to this planet. He was determined to discover who sought him, and to know the reason. All through the night, he lay thinking, considering all the possibilities, considering all his options.

The morning came with a sudden splash of brilliant orange, followed by the usual flashes of bright white light interspersed with red and green bolts of lightning, as the heat from the sun ignited the gases high above the ordinary atmosphere. As the jagged shards of multicolored bolts of light split across the horizon, they painted the faces of the early morning watchers with a golden hue. Mornings were always a beautiful spectacle.

"I hear your friend stirring," said Jules quietly.

"I know. Let him awaken alone. He will soon rise." Cubal continued to watch the incredible display of light. In the forest, this display had been all but invisible. Here, just beyond the city, the sky was open, and he stood marveling at the morning explosions.

In a few minutes, the young man emerged from the small hut. He smiled as he saw Cubal and held out his hand in a curious fashion. The other two watched as the man and Cubal exchanged greetings. Finally, the other said, "I seem to have fallen prey to kidnappers."

Cubal nodded. "You were taken to the world of the A'rkji. I went with you. They decided they did not want to eat us, so we came back."

The young man's smile was wide and he looked at the other two. "Do these friends of yours know of what you speak?"

Jules said, "We know. We also know that when he came back with you, there were seven A'rkji soldiers, plus one small A'rkji who had returned with both of you on the shining plate. The seven soldiers went back with the one, but the seven did not know of their return."

"I wonder that there were any to return to on A'rkji." The young man stared knowingly at Cubal. He knew the ways of this man well.

The warrior was quiet for a long moment, then said softly: "Their king and I have a peace agreement. They will never again seek human prey." He turned his gaze back to the sky.

Antal said quickly, "And what did they get in return?" Before an answer could come, he blinked as understanding came to him. He laughed heartily, then said, "Of course. Existence is something even they understand."

The young man moved closer to Cubal. "What brings you to this place, my friend?"

Cubal countered with a question. "You are far from home as well, Blythe the Seeker. What brought you to become the featured course at the A'rkji banquet?"

The young man took a deep breath and said, "I was assigned to this planet by one of our officials to set up a new trade arrangement.

However, privately, my father asked me to seek answers about a matter of concern on our planet that apparently has some connections to this place. Once here, I was instructed by two of the officials to go to the Halls of K'bla. They said that there were men who knew the answers to my questions. But, it is clear to me, now, that the purpose of those who sent me was to insure I came in contact with the A'rkji. When I came within close proximity of the A'rkji, they grabbed me, beat me, and then I was suddenly with you on their planet."

Cubal said, "I tried to remove you, but I could not get you off in time. It was a good thing, though, because it enabled me to persuade the king of the A'rkji to have peace with all of mankind." A tiny smile lifted one corner of his mouth.

Cubal continued, "I also persuaded their king to return us." The smiled disappeared. He peered intently at his friend and said, "But what information do you seek, Blythe?"

"I seek to know more about Barth, the Bearded One."

"Who is he?"

"He is Counselor to my father, and now, even more than that. He has been a busy man and has made himself important in the Ministry of Resources. Do you know what that means?"

Cubal was silent for a long moment. "I know it means that one in his position can do many things that can be destructive to your world, if he is not a careful man."

Blythe nodded. "He is not a careful man, Cubal." He wiped at his face and added, "He is from Earth, and I believe him to be a trader whose base was here in Na'ha. Indeed, if my information is correct, not just a trader, but a dishonest trader, one who used to trade in the forbidden spices of Yod'lun. He was called Laird at one time."

Cubal instantly frowned. He knew the name. He said, "This is serious, Blythe. You must return home quickly, and I must go with you. I know this man, and I can assure you that he is extremely dangerous."

The young man's eyes widened and he said, "You would do this? Ah, my friend, this is more than fortune. This is a God event."

Cubal laughed. "You still follow that old belief in a God of the Universe—this ancient concept of the one called Yeshua or Messiah, I believe you called him?"

Blythe nodded. "I do. I have not changed since we last met." He was quiet for a long moment, then added, "You would follow my belief, too, my friend, if ever you had visited Earth and met with Yeshua, our Messiah-King, ruler of the universe and all that is."

"But, my friend, I did visit there, once, just before he ended his rule. And, while I did not meet this god-king of yours, I did see much of the world he ruled before he left it."

Cubal paused for a long moment, hesitant about continuing the conversation, not wanting to offend, but also wanting to take the opening offered him by the other. Finally, he said softly, "If your king, this Yeshua or Messiah, or whatever name you call him, if he were truly this powerful god of whom you speak, he would not have left his place to another. Since his departure, many have sought his throne, and wars have erupted on Earth. You know that I fought in those early wars. So, my friend, I've seen too many wars to hold to a belief that your Messiah rules the Universe. Indeed, he could not even continue to rule a single planet."

Cubal's tone was friendly, not mocking. He understood the importance of his friend's belief, and while he could not accept that belief, he knew it was a reality to Blythe. But, he could not pass the opportunity to show his friend a glaring error in his belief. Whatever else this Messiah might be, the fact remained that he'd surrendered his throne and left for another world.

Blythe smiled at his friend. "This was all known long beforehand. You make an assumption that is incorrect when you say he abandoned his throne. He yet rules, even on Earth. The time of testing of the world, yea, even in the heavens, has come. These things were foretold."

Cubal permitted the ghost of a smile to come to his lips as he said, "I am sorry, friend, but your god sounds as though he was having some difficulties ruling his kingdom. He does not sound like much of a god to me. The Kasdeons have ruled with impunity for well over two thousand years. This one ruled for what, a thousand or so of Earth years?"

"Yes, but as I said, He has not abandoned Earth."

Cubal merely smiled and did not reply, but moved his gaze from his friend to the now docile sky above, signaling his desire to cease the conversation. He knew the belief system fairly well. He'd been trained in almost all the religious rites and systems on Earth, and had also studied hundreds of alien religious belief systems. The system called Christianity was the one that most intrigued him, for it was the one most documented, and it had the most unusual history. Also, it was of earthly origin, unlike so many that had their roots in the stars with alien forms who, because of different powers, had been able to convince others they were gods. He knew Christianity's strengths and its weaknesses, understood the foundations of the belief, and knew why he could never accept such a system of belief.

Many of its prophets had long foretold of the demise of mankind and of the end of this evil being they'd called Satan, and of the ultimate kingdom of the one they called Messiah. But, life had continued for thousands of years, and except for the brief period of time when this one called Messiah, or someone claiming to be him, had actually ruled upon Earth, there had been no kingdom established of which Cubal was aware.

During the rule of this Messiah-king, mankind had conquered the intricacies of space travel. There had been great leaps in technological and medical knowledge during his rule. No star was too distant. No world was too foreign. Disease was conquered, and life expectancy on Earth was said to be similar to the days of Earth's earliest history when men and women lived hundreds of years. Although the stories of the King called Jesus, a man who'd suddenly appeared on the planet and took over after a major war, were astounding, they did not convince Cubal of his divinity. He was merely another of those beings who had some special powers and abilities. Indeed, he was such a being himself.

*And I know I am no god, but merely a man destined to die one day, probably in a battle.*

His thoughts turned to the last wars in which he'd played a part. The entire human race had come close to extinction soon after the departure of this Messiah king. Some would attribute the saving of humankind to those like Cubal, but he knew that was not true. It is true that he and others like him had attacked the home world of the beings called Crs'tings, but that was not what had caused them to cease their war with humans. He was certain of that. They'd left Earth for reasons he had never been able to discern.

These strange creatures had been able, somehow, to adapt and change their shapes and their molecular structure to match almost perfectly, a particular human, and they'd had learned how to incorporate the actual DNA of that individual. Some of them had even been able to meld the thought patterns of a targeted human into their being. Cubal had found himself fighting a clone of himself on two occasions. The first time, victory had been easy. It had been unsettling seeing himself so perfectly formed, moving in ways that were far too close to his own movements. However, that first Crs'ting had not moved with the speed and grace of a Wearer of the Black.

But the second one had been different. Cubal had sensed that from the beginning. Every move Cubal had made had been countered. It was a struggle with himself. It had been a long, ardous battle, each warrior tiring at the same moment and backing away to regain strength, to find a weakness, a flaw, something that was not in his pattern of thought nor in his genetic makeup, nor his training. There had been only one tiny difference between them. The alien being required all data to flow through some small portion of its mind where it maintained its own peculiar identity. That required a few milliseconds of time which slowed the creature slightly.

Because it was such a small bit of time, Cubal could not take advantage of it until the seventeenth minute of the battle. He'd learned of the small difference of speed in the first minute, but could not seem to take advantage of the difference. Finally, in the last minute, he'd performed a maneuver that he'd never made, nor would he have considered in other circumstances since it did expose him for an entire micro-second of time. It required all of his focus, all of his strength, and all of his speed. The only way for the other to avoid death in this move was to move in perfect unison and strike at the brief micro-second when he was vulnerable. The difference in speed became noticeable to Cubal after three seconds into the maneuver. Too late, the alien realized his slowness and could neither take advantage of the opening, nor avoid the blow that destroyed it.

Almost immediately after the death of this Crs'ting clone of Cubal, the strange beings had retreated from the Earth, and even from the other worlds they'd conquered and absorbed. Most returned to their home planet to defend it, while millions hid themselves amongst obscure dwellings in the stars.

In the beginning of the wars with the Crs'tings, the death toll had been on a scale never known in the history of any planet. Millions of Crs'tings had died, but so had many other species, both human and alien. Near the end, after his battle with the clone, because of the scale of the operations and the enormous losses, the Crs'tings had withdrawn its armies from other worlds, and those troops were sent to the home planet for its defense. They'd abandoned Earth almost completely. He knew some had remained there because there had been reports he'd read which seemed to indicate that some Crs'tings had remained integrated into the human species there. There was no way to detect them by the ordinary human.

Cubal had seen those new Crs'ting arrivals in the war years, some fresh from Earth itself, looking as human as himself. It was this group, the ones from Earth, who had perfected the cloning techniques. Clearly, they'd been studying mankind on Earth, analyzing the subatomic structures of man, the DNA, and more. They'd studied brain waves, and had somehow managed to clone humans almost perfectly. *Almost.* There was always that sense of alien about them. Cubal could sense it. There was something missing. Every Crs'ting he'd encountered had an alien presence to it. All of the Wearers of the Black could distinguish between a real human and a Crs'ting. But, ordinary humans could not do that. He'd never met one human who could tell the difference.

But, it was not the carnage caused by the Wearers of the Black that had stopped these aliens. Cubal knew that. While the Crs'ting armies had suffered enormous losses, they still were winning many battles, and because of the cloning, had been able to infiltrate high levels of Earth's military and political structures. He was not sure why they'd suddenly retreated and hidden themselves. Whatever or whoever it was, they'd been frightened. These aliens, who'd shown no fear, suddenly ran for hiding places like children afraid of a storm. Why? It was but one of a myriad of mysteries Cubal had in his experiences as a warrior and a wanderer of the universe.

But he did not have questions about a Messiah.

45

*There is no savior of mankind.* His thought was heavy with belief, clad with the armor of his nearly two hundred years of experience in life. He had seen no such saviour. He had seen no gods intervening. The closest thing to a god was himself and others like him who fought in the wars that came after this Messiah-being left Earth.

While some declared that this being still occupied Earth, Cubal doubted it. Most of the reliable reports he'd seen and heard, told of a dramatic change upon the Earth. Prior to that, Earth had been the most peaceful planet in the galaxy, and was impressive for so many reasons. There were no wars, no disease, and no criminal activity on the entire planet. That was no longer true. Cubal could only conclude that this being had either died, or for reasons unknown, had abandoned the planet.

There was no question that a being named Jesus, who claimed to be Messiah, a god of the people called Jews, had walked ancient Earth. The Stone Viewers had determined that much. It was not absolutely clear that the one who'd walked ancient Earth was the same being who'd controlled Earth for a thousand of Earth years, but much of the evidence suggested they were one and the same. And, there was little doubt that this being once called Christ, had powers that were unlike any that those people could have imagined in that day. The history had been verified, as well as his apparent death which had occurred on two pieces of wood fastened together and placed in a hole in the ground.

Moreover, by use of a Rocktime Spectrometer—a device used for viewing historical data from ancient rocks—they'd been able to surmise that this creature had somehow managed to revive itself after three days. The images clearly showed the creature—whether human or not, Cubal did not know, though it had appeared to be human— awakening after three days lying on a stone in apparent death. But, Cubal understood that these things were possible for certain men who were trained to have absolute control over their bodies. They could feign death such that only the most sensitive instruments could detect life. It was something he had been trained to do as well.

As to the healings and such, there were some he knew who had powers over the flesh so as to control disease, and even heal others. It was an art that he was acquainted with and could duplicate to some degree. He could not revive one in whom the life force was truly gone, though. And, it was said that this being did that. Cubal doubted that was true.

He doubted that the one called Christ by the Jews, who'd lived in those early years of Earth's history, and the one they called King, who'd ruled Earth for a thousand years, were the same beings. Possible, but not likely, even though life spans had greatly increased during the Millennium, and it was not uncommon for one to live hundreds of years.

But, even if it were so, that this Christ was alive thousands of years earlier than his reign on Earth, it was of no great significance to Cubal. Longevity was found in other beings, and even humans in their early history had recorded life spans of hundreds of years. He knew of some alien life forms with life spans of more than a thousand years. No, the truth was likely that the being they called Christ, and the king who'd ruled Earth, were two remarkable beings with unusual powers. Nothing more.

"Cubal? May we leave now?" Blythe stood staring at his silent friend who'd stood in quiet contemplation for several long minutes, staring into the sky.

Cubal smiled. "Of course. Have you a transport?"

"I suppose I do. I left it with the Trader Landing Authority."

Cubal nodded. "It will be there. There are many strange things and stranger ways on this planet, but one thing they do is protect the traveler's ships. It will be there even if you perish, and it will remain until you or your heirs come to claim it."

The four headed back toward the city, Cubal leading the small band. No one but the black-cloaked warrior seemed to notice the small, almost invisible light hovering high above them. As they moved down a small trail, he detected movement far ahead of them. Someone was taking great pains to insure that they hid themselves. He doubted anyone had noticed the movement but himself. But, he did not underestimate Antal. That one had surprised him too many times.

They came to a small bend in the trail when Cubal saw the blur of a force field suddenly leap across the trail, just in front of him.

As he whirled around, a second field shot across the trail, cutting him off from the rest of the group.

He held his hands up, facing Blythe and the others. "Stay where you are. There is a force field here. I will be safe. Do not attempt to interfere. The one who seeks me comes. I will return soon. Please remain here and be vigilant."

Suddenly, a blue light shot from a ship that appeared just above Cubal. The warrior disappeared. Antal shouted, "Where did he go?"

Blythe said softly, "He will return. Let us rest beside the trail under those trees." He pointed to a small clearing and a stand of trees that offered shade. Antal and Jules stood for several moments staring at the now empty sky, then moved to join Blythe who seated himself under a large tree.

Far away, in the city, a small ship shimmered into a visible shape as it floated down a long, tube-like apparatus. It docked within a huge building. Inside, Cubal stood, arms folded. He would now learn who hunted him. He could have avoided capture, and even now, could escape. But, it would be easier this way. He had permitted the hunter to catch the prey. That hunter would learn the danger of making prey of a Wearer of the Black.

The door to the ship whooshed open and immediately, Cubal stepped out into a large room. He was surrounded by more than 100 soldiers, all armed with various weapons, none of them appearing to be lethal. Many were armed with Beryl lassos, a few with Beryl whips, and some with stun clubs. One had a sound weapon used to immobilize a victim, and he spotted three with hand-held force field devices that could immobilize a man for several minutes. If one was held longer than a few minutes in its grip, he died.

"Cubal, you will not be harmed. I have been asked to deliver you to Earth unharmed. Will you resist? If you do, I have weapons that will incapacitate you." Ka'tre of L'trel stood on an elevated walkway above the room, clad in a dark grey suit with a narrow, yellow stripe running down the left side, indicating his high position of rank on the planet.

Cubal was not surprised that a government official sought him, but it did arouse his curiosity. He wondered who was powerful enough to reach all the way from Earth to command an official of Na'ha to capture him.

"Who seeks me?" The question was a command, and he used his special powers to project his words into the mind of the other. He saw the slender man-like being wince as the words impacted his mind.

"The Ancient Ones of Earth."

"And who are you?"

There was a brief hesitation, then the being replied boldly, "I am Ka'tre of L'trel."

Cubal turned his head slowly to his left as his gaze took in all of the soldiers, then turned to look upon the others. He turned slowly and viewed those who encircled him.

Finally, he turned to face the one called Ka'tre and said, "Do you comprehend that I am able to destroy all who stand in this room and that there is no weapon here that can prevent me from doing that?"

Ka'tre felt fear rising up in him, then quenched the fear as his mind filled with the thoughts of the weapon he'd acquired and of the reward that would be his once he delivered the warrior. He cleared his throat and said, "I know of your prowess, warrior. I ask that you come peacefully."

"I will not go with you." Cubal was tempted, but once he'd learned who sought him, he'd decided instantly he would go to them, but on his own terms and in his own time.

"Then you leave me with no choice." Suddenly, the man pressed a button on a device clutched in one hand and instantly, the entire room was filled with a greenish haze. Every soldier crumpled to the floor.

Cubal remained standing, arms folded, staring intently at Ka'tre.

Then suddenly, he was standing next to Ka'tre, and he propelled the government official through a small door. The door whispered closed and he slid across the polished floor where Cubal had tossed him. Ka'tre raised himself to a sitting position, then removed the small filters hidden in his nostrils.

"How could you withstand the effects of Q'uria? Nothing in the files suggested you could do that? Even the Ancient Ones did not think you could withstand that, if it were delivered quickly."

Cubal ignored the question, and instead walked up close to the man and said, "Ka'tre of L'trel, I will spare your life this day. If ever I sense that you hunt me again, I shall come for you and crush your life force." He spoke with the authority and command only one trained in the voice and mind techniques of D'vru could speak.

Ka'tre blinked once, then whispered, "I have been the fool. Never again shall I hunt one such as you in my existence." It was an existence that was now made very tenuous by his failure. Those who'd assigned him the task did not overlook failure.

He watched as the man clad in the dark cloak left the room unchallenged.

*Where can I hide from them?* The thought was like a sliver of ice in his brain.

The answer came to him as quickly as the thought of hiding: *No one can hide from the Ancient Ones.*

# Chapter 6

*"The cunning of an opponent is not to be measured by its intelligence. Evaluate your enemy's cunning by knowing his weakness, his level of fear, and his regard for life—not just his own."* D'VRU, BOOK TWO: *The Measure of Life*

They stood at the center of the anti-grav field where thousands of transports rested quietly, no signs of life around them. The Transport Deputy stepped off the small circle that had risen to the field level with them and moved onto the field itself.

"Your machine is there." He pointed toward a long row of identical transports, and instantly a small circle of lights went on around one of the transports. The deputy handed Blythe a small cylinder which served as identification of Blythe to the transport system. "May all your travels be as your visit with us, sir." With that, he gave a little bow, then turned and marched crisply back to the circle, stepped upon the lift and with a wave of the hand, descended out of sight.

Blythe chuckled and said under his breath, "Let's hope not."

The four moved toward the transport. Antal walked slowly, lingering behind. After a bit, he stopped and called out, "I do not wish to make this journey."

Cubal had sensed the fear rising in the man as they'd walked. He turned to Antal and said, "Your fear is well taken. There awaits a mystery for you there, but answers as well. It is good that you fear. But, it is not good that you stay. You must journey."

The big man hesitated then said, "You are right. I am acting as a child."

The men stepped into the transport. Cubal selected the large, supple chair next to the Operations Panel. Blythe took the seat next to his, then began speaking in a low monotone voice. A soft voice that seemed to drift from somewhere within the walls of the vessel spoke: "Welcome Blythe. It has been seven lights and four times of dimming since you have boarded. Where are you destined?"

"Home. Just home."

"As soon as your passengers restrict their movements, I will begin the sequencing."

Cubal waved one hand at the two wary men who stood looking around the small vessel with all the caution of a suspicious animal, wary of its surroundings, unwilling to trust its senses. "Sit, my friends. There is nothing to fear. There will be a small moment of discomfort. That will be the transport moving us inter-dimensionally, and then, in just a few minutes, we will arrive. It will only take a few moments of your time, though you will travel beyond hundreds of years of your life."

The two men sat in the large seats toward the rear of the vessel. As soon as each sat down, the chair enveloped them in its embrace. Antal's eyes widened, and his instincts bade him leap from the chair, but he resisted the urge. Jules stared at his friend for a long moment, then relaxed in the embrace of the chair, confident that his friend Cubal would not have brought him into danger. But, it did not lessen the nervous feeling in his stomach.

There was a brilliant flash of blue-white light, and all felt a sudden, sickening feeling in the pit of their stomach. They were moving, yet not moving. There were no vibrations and no sense of movement, but it was apparent that they were no longer on the planet. Through the slitted visor ahead, there was a blur of lights and color surrounding them.

Suddenly, the lights vanished and the insides of the small ship were brightened with a golden glow from the brilliant bluish-orange light of a strange sun. "We are here. Let's go and see who will come to visit with us." Blythe stood and the four exited the vessel, with Blythe leading, Cubal behind him, while Jules and Antal followed in subdued silence.

They were greeted by two Transportation Agents who led them to a large room that glowed with a blue-green light. They were instructed to be seated in one of the many large, seats that ringed the entire room. For nearly an hour, they sat waiting. Blythe appeared serene, in spite of the delay, but it was obvious that he was not pleased. After awhile, he stood, walked to a view port and peered through the window for a long minute, then returned to his seat.

"Something is wrong, Cubal. My father would have sent for us by now. He would not keep us waiting like this."

Cubal smiled softly and said, "It is why I returned with you, friend. If Laird is here, then your entire planet is in danger."

Blythe's eyes narrowed. "What do you know of this man?"

Cubal took a deep breath and raised his head to the stars as the memories flooded his mind. He spoke in a low monotone, his face to the ceiling. "He comes bearing gifts and is one possessed of many skills. He can be a charming man, loves to speak to great crowds, and seems able to ingratiate himself to those he befriends. He will bring things to a planet that he knows they need, and will even give these things as gifts, in exchange for a position within the government. He lands alone, but commands an unseen army to do his bidding. It is said that his origins are of Earth. I do not know. I do know he is human."

Cubal folded his arms across his chest, then continued, "Once he instills himself into the inner workings of a planet's government, he works to take control. When he is able to gain enough control to land his forces, he then begins the completion of his ultimate goal: the stripping of the planet of its wealth and its people. No doubt, he has, or will soon set up a space corridor on the planet. Probably, he will establish several of them. There will be a ship out there somewhere to receive the people and re-transport them to whoever is paying the highest price."

He looked at Blythe and concluded, "Laird is a raider of planets and he has come to strip your planet of its wealth and its people."

Blythe said softly, "This man must be stopped."

"He will not harm anyone, yet. If I am correct, he is here to first place himself in a position of authority. He will have gradually imported some of his soldiers. He is known to have waited a dozen years to take over a planet. Laird has not yet completely seized control of the planet."

Blythe asked, "How do you know this?"

"I observe. There are too many things in place that are yet normal. Once he seizes absolute control, there will be no resemblance to the old system. At this point, I would suspect he only has control of one part of your government and...."

Cubal's voice trailed off. He held his hand up for silence, then whispered, "Whatever you do, make no resistance. Let them do with us what they wish for the moment. They will have no interest in killing us for we are valuable to them alive and worthless dead."

An armed body of soldiers in midnight blue came through the door that whooshed open. Cubal noticed instantly they were armed with small, beam-radzers, hand-held weapons that could cut through the hull of space craft from a distance of ten feet. Its effective range on living organisms was nearly a mile, and its accuracy was not dependent on the user. If one pointed in the general direction, within a foot of the target, it was set to seek the warmth radiated by life, and its rays would actually bend toward the prey. Cubal knew the ways of the weapon and could evade it, but few others could.

The soldiers moved apart, and one large man with no visible weapon stepped from behind the soldiers. "You are Blythe. You will come with me. Your father is expecting you."

"My friends are with me. We will go together."

The man hesitated for a moment, then shrugged. "As you wish."

At that, he turned, and the soldiers fell in behind the four. Antal was stripped rudely of his weapons, which he surrendered with a growl. Cubal's almost imperceptible nod of his head kept the big man under control. Jules surrendered his spear and knives without hesitation. He was not afraid. He'd seen what these soldiers had not seen.

*They have never seen a Bora tiger.* He smiled at the thought.

Cubal moved out ahead, following the large soldier. He said softly to the others, "Life is secure. Do not fear."

In a few minutes, the group reached what Cubal recognized as the Hall of The Just Ones. It was here that all judging was done, and the President's office was on this floor. It was in this place Cubal had first met Blythe. They were escorted into one of the huge arena rooms. As they entered, Cubal sensed danger within the room. He also felt the vibrations of a space corridor somewhere nearby.

*He is nearly ready to begin stripping the planet.* Cubal knew Laird would likely attempt to send himself and his friends to a waiting ship where they would then be sent to as slaves to a mining colony.

They were stopped in the center of the room. On a large throne-like chair sat a massive, bearded man. Cubal recognized the man as Laird. It had been a long time since he'd seen Laird, and he wondered if the man would recognize him. Their encounter had been brief, for the man had been escorted from a planet where Cubal, and two like himself, had destroyed the entire armies of Laird and a man called Ryel, who'd been second in command.

Cubal had stood in the shadows as Laird had been escorted to a transport. The big, burly man had paused for a long moment as he'd passed, and he'd stared into the shadows at Cubal, then soldiers had shoved him into the transport device. Later, Cubal heard the man had managed to escape his captors while working the mines on an obscure moon.

He wasn't surprised. Laird had the ability of an Earth chameleon, and could adapt into virtually any role he chose to play with convincing candor and believability. The man had pretended to be a guard and had simply commandeered a small Security vessel. It had taken them weeks to even discover he was missing, since he'd concocted an elaborate scheme that had him supposedly working the outer edges of the moon for an extended period of time.

The four stood there in the center of the room for several minutes, the quietness of the huge room adding to the feeling of danger. Cubal could see Laird speaking to someone standing in the shadows just out of sight, beside him, but the sound was muffled in the great hall.

Suddenly, Laird spoke: "Greetings, Blythe! It is good that you have come home. Your father has missed you."

Blythe was silent.

"What, no wonderment about your father?" The big man laughed and then continued, "No matter. You will see him soon. But, it is business first." He whispered into the darkness beside him and then turned back and in his gruff, deep voice, said, "Tell us of your friends. Who are they and from what planet do they come?"

Cubal stepped forward and said, "These are simple hunters from Na'ha, and I am but a traveler who chanced upon them and invited them to travel with us."

"And your name, stranger?" Laird was intensely curious now, leaning forward in his seat.

"I am called by the name Caleb." It was true, for at birth, Cubal was called Caleb, and had been so called until the tenth year of his life. It was a name he chose to use from time-to-time as he deemed convenient.

"Well, Caleb, what event occurred to have you traveling with the son of the president of this planet?"

"I was acquainted with Blythe many years ago. We chanced to meet on Na'ha. He invited me to return with him." Cubal's senses were alerting him to danger, and it was becoming more difficult for him to maintain the docile, weak and helpless appearance, for he knew there was a serious danger to himself in that room, but he could not tell from who, or what, or where, the danger lay.

A soft voice came from the darkness, and instantly, Cubal knew why he'd sensed danger to himself. "Cubal pretending to be a mere mortal? How interesting." The speaker emerged from the shadows.

"Hello Butre. It has been many wars since last we worked together. Apparently, you have forgotten the words of our way, which says, 'Service to evil brings a weakness that blinds the eye and slows the mind.' Are you here to subdue and conquer?"

"I work where I am able. At the moment, I work for a consortium that needs labor." He paused for a long moment, then added, "But, my old friend, we will not be seeking your labors. It would be an impossible task, so you may go, and you may take your friends along as well."

"What do you mean he may go!" demanded Laird. "You do not give the orders on this planet. These are men worth much as laborers.

They are strong and will last." The man's voice trembled as he spoke, the anger evident, as he gestured vigorously with his hands.

He turned his head back to Cubal and said, "Whoever you are, Caleb or whoever, understand this: I rule this planet. You will be taken to a place and there exchanged for a sum that will guarantee you a long life of work. Indeed, You may never need to look for work again as long as you live." Cubal caught a glimpse of the flash of the man's gleaming white teeth as he smiled.

Suddenly, the soft laughter of the one in the shadows sounded and Laird whirled around and snarled at the one called Butre, "You think to mock me? Though you wear the black and are feared by many, you are not invincible. If I must, I can end our relationship."

Butre stepped forward into the light. He did not appear to have taken offense at the words of Laird. He extended one arm, and the black cloak swept aside as he said, "Allow me to complete introductions. Laird, meet Cubal, destroyer of worlds, a Wearer of the Black, and warrior supreme. I believe you have met him once before." The smile was on the man's face and in his voice. He was enjoying the moment.

The shock on Laird's face was apparent to all. He shrank back, visibly shaken. He peered intently at Cubal, his memory rushing like the wind, flooding his mind with the images of death he'd seen of his vaunted army, almost all of them slain by one man: *this man*. And, he recalled seeing this man standing in the shadows as he was led away by the Universal Security Force.

*It cannot be. No! It cannot be!* The denial was a shout of thought that flashed through his mind.

"You are that man?" he asked, his voice husky with emotion.

Cubal no longer postured himself in a shrunken, helpless fashion, but instead, stood now as the proud and strong warrior he was, unafraid of any being. He stepped forward and said, "I see you have escaped and returned to plunder worlds. And now, you do it with the aid of one who wears the black. But, you've chosen to raid the world of a friend. While some who wear the black have forgotten their teachings about never serving an evil master, not all who wear the black have forgotten."

Laird was silent a long moment, then said, his voice weak. "I am not a stupid man. I recall our last meeting. But, I have one here who is your equal, and more. He will compel you to work or to die." He turned to Butre and pointed.

Butre laughed. "Laird, for this one and myself to battle in this room would probably bring death to all present, including yourself. Is that what you want? I do not fear Cubal, but I cannot claim I am his equal. I do not know of anyone who was ever his equal, excepting perhaps one, and he has perished in the wars with the Crs'ting."

Laird replied, his voice cracking, "Deal with this man. It is what I pay you to do." Fear had filled his entire being. He rose quickly, moved toward the back of the room, then disappeared into an adjacent room, his fear driving him. He did not want to be that close to the two most dangerous men he'd ever met, especially if they began fighting. He knew that his only hope of escape was for Butre to engage the warrior, perhaps distract him, and hopefully defeat him. He sat heavily into a chair, trembling, uncertain as to what to do, but unwilling to abandon the riches that were so close to being his.

Butre shrugged and turned to Cubal. "It is not my wish to engage you. We would do injury to one another, perhaps one of us would prevail, perhaps not. It is likely that I would injure you, but you would probably destroy me. It is better that you and your friends should leave. We will give you free passage."

"It is not that simple, Butre. You have chosen a dark path and darker masters. I cannot permit you to strip this world of its citizens."

Butre smiled. "I assumed you'd take that position. That's why I prepared for your coming when I received word from Na'ha that you were arriving."

Cubal was instantly into the fifth level of his discipline. It was not something he thought about consciously, but was a state of being that he sometimes slipped into when he was about to do battle. It was as though there was something deep within him that told him at what level in his sub-consciousness that he must reach exist in order to survive. Normally, rising to the fifth level was something he only went to when he had been on certain missions where there was danger surrounding him on different levels, from different sources, and of different intensities. His battle with the Crs'tings had demanded that level, and once, even more.

Butre moved back into the shadows. Cubal was already moving with a speed that defied ordinary human ability. He propelled his friends towards the entrance of the room. In seconds, he'd thrust them through the doors, then whirled to meet the death he knew was already upon him.

It came in the form of a lithe, stick-thin creature known in the universe for its deadliness. One touch by this creature, called Dre'so, and death came in the form of paralysis of every organ. But, Cubal knew this would not be the only seeker of his life. This deadly creature was merely a diversion. Butre would send this one, and while engaged in battle with the Dre'so, someone, or something else, would be sent, and then another, and as many as it took to bring death to him.

But, Butre had never progressed completely in the ways of D'vru, and had not mastered all of its levels. Cubal had. Butre had reached his limits, and although far superior to almost any other being, he had not come to know completely, the ways of D'vru. Indeed, to the knowledge of Cubal, only himself and one other had ever gone beyond the sixth level, and he was fairly certain that other one had died in the Crs'ting wars. Ma'jor had never been seen by anyone after a particularly vicious battle. It was said that this warrior had personally destroyed over 23,000 Crs'tings in a months-long battle. This was the one spoken of by Butre.

The Dre'so creature felt nothing but wind as it struck at its prey, and then its entire being was shattered into thousands of pieces as a force that it would never have understood enveloped it and crushed it until its frame shattered. Cubal had not touched the creature, for to touch it was to invite the strange venom from it into one's system. Every warrior trained in the ways of D'vru knew of the powers of the spirit-mind, something once called *Ki* by those who'd practiced its use on Earth thousands of years before. But, Cubal's powers went far beyond merely sending a blow of pure energy to the enemy. He knew how to shape that force, to focus it, and use it as men use their hands.

The battle with the creature lasted barely two seconds. Instantly, a door whooshed open and three dark-clad figures swept into the room.

Their smell identified them as Crailians, strong, resilient fighters from the planet Crail. They were of the warrior class and knew no fear, not even from a Wearer of the Black. Their danger lay in their absolute mastery of virtually every fighting technique known in the universe. They'd even managed to emulate some of the techniques of D'vru.

Cubal knew they'd lingered too long in waiting, but understood why they'd waited. They knew that even an accidental brush against the Dre'so creature would bring death to them. He wondered if Butre had told them they would be fighting a Wearer of the Black. He suspected they'd not been told. The three were a team, trained from birth to kill. Death was their only trade. They were paid well for their work and had long mastered their art.

The trio moved into the room using the Sneith pattern, moves that were common to that discipline, and one especially useful for team attacks. Cubal became instantly aware that all of this was not as it seemed. Butre knew him well enough to know that none of these creatures would be able to kill him. Butre's plan was much deeper.

*He seeks to distract me.* Cubal's mind raced as he sorted out the possibilities, even as one part of him parried the moves of the death team now circling him.

One alien swept in from the side, clinging close to the floor. Cubal knew the second fighter would be leaping high into the air, and the third would rush from the front, then leap to the rear, joining the one in the air who was to have landed behind Cubal. It was almost as though he could read their minds, their moves were so transparent to him.

He whirled and leaped into the air, meeting the startled being who was descending. One blow, and that creature fell in a crumpled heap. Cubal landed several feet away. He looked up at where he'd last seen Butre. He wondered idly what the real attack would be, and when, and where. His eyes swept the room, his senses fully extended. He could detect no movement, no strange life forces, and no radiant threats.

Suddenly, he parried the laser beam of one of the Crailians with a small diamond mirror concealed in the palm of his hand. One flick of his hand sent the beam back into the sender's eyes. The Crailian screamed in pain and dropped to the floor. The third warrior stood still. He'd quit his attack the moment he'd seen the first companion slain and realized what manner of being they were fighting. They'd not been told they'd be fighting a Wearer of the Black, and especially, not this particular one. He knew this warrior, and had once seen him fight during the Crs'ting wars.

He'd seen the Dre'so slain, and then, his two companions destroyed by a man who almost seemed distracted by the entire thing. He knew that to advance on this warrior was to die, and while he was not afraid, he also did not wish to die as a fool. Clearly, they'd not been told all that was needed to be told about this job.

He held out his hands, palm upwards, in a universal sign of peace and said, "I seek not your life, Cubal, Wearer of the Black. Let us have peace."

Cubal barely acknowledged him as he said softly, "Leave quickly. I will do you no harm." The man retreated and disappeared through the small entrance from which he'd emerged just moments ago. Cubal waited. He knew there would come another attack, and he sensed that it would be from a weapon of some sort.

He was not disappointed. Suddenly, the room became bright, as though lit by an unseen sun, and instantly a spidery web of light surrounded him. He did not move, sensing that the device was not to harm him, but only to restrain him. He prepared himself for the maneuver he'd practiced so many times before while in the mountains of Na'ha. He would use the dimensional shifting technique to move himself from the web of light and toward the shadowy figure he knew was Butre.

Suddenly, a voice filled the room. He froze in place instantly. The voice was with a tone and level of command that he'd never heard before, similar to that of the authority voice level used by himself and others trained in the use of the voice in that way. It freezes the opponent momentarily because its power rivets the attention of the hearer. He had thought himself immune to the technique. It is an energy of the mind more than the actual voice, that is sent to another, though the voice level and intensity is an essential part of the technique. The difference in this voice was that it was on a level much higher than he'd ever heard or used. And, he knew the voice.

*Blythe? How can this be?*

"Do not move! I will explain to you later. You will harm yourself if you attempt to go through the field." The urgency and command in the voice was too great for Cubal to ignore. He relaxed and took himself out of the mind-set preparatory to a shift.

Blythe stepped through the open door and moved into the center of the room. He looked at Butre and said, "Release him." The command was pure energy, wrapped in words and delivered with a force that even Cubal could feel physically.

He watched as Butre staggered back, affected visibly by the command, clutching at his head. He gasped, "Who are you? What is this power you possess that permits you to explode your words in my head?"

Blythe did not reply but watched the other steadily, his gaze not wavering.

Slowly, Butre reached down to his belt and pressed something. Instantly, the web disappeared.

Blythe spoke, with his voice now in a control level used to influence a mind, but somehow different. Cubal sensed the power in the voice as he spoke: "You will remove yourself, Laird, and all those who came with you, from this planet. Leave the seven transport devices you have. Do not attempt to take them. If you are not gone from here within one hour, you will all be destroyed."

Butre started to reply, then stopped. Something had happened to him, and although he did not understand it, he knew that to dispute with this being was to embrace death. Blythe had done something to him that even Cubal had not been able to do: he was afraid. He could not recall the last time he'd been afraid, but knew it had been as a child. A chill swept over him as he moved back into the room where Laird had hidden.

*It is true, the stories. This is a dangerous, forbidden place.* His mind conceded what he'd dismissed as fables.

Laird was cowering in a chair in one corner, awaiting the outcome, unsure of who would be walking through the door. A large hand was wiping sweat off his brow when Butre entered. He leaped up at the sight of Butre. "Is he dead?" he exclaimed.

Butre sneered at the man. "No, and we must leave this place instantly or we will all be dead. We have one hour to leave this planet with our men. What was told me years ago about this planet is true. It is a forbidden place."

"Leave? What are you talking about? I cannot leave! I will not leave."

Butre had no time to waste with the man. He whirled and grabbed the big man by the throat and lifted him effortlessly into the air. His words, rich with resonance, and commanding in tone, were delivered in a clipped, crisp voice. "If you do not issue the order to immediately depart, I will kill you here and now. You fool, I do not have time to explain it nor to debate it. But, if you value your life, you will order your men to the shuttles now. Send those who are near the transport devices through the transports. We can gather them onto the proper vessels later." He dropped Laird and headed for the door.

"But what about the transports? They must be dismantled. That will take a day."

"Leave them! I tell you there is no time to waste. If we are here in less than an hour, we are all dead men."

The absolute surety in Butre's voice convinced Laird that he could not afford to doubt the man. This strange man with the scarred face was a Wearer of the Black, and to see this man fear for his life could only mean that there was a real danger of his dying if he stayed or delayed. He'd been on two worlds with this man and had seen him destroy some of those worlds' fiercest warriors. There had never been even a flicker of fear in the man. Until now.

*What happened to him?* He saw fear in a man who knew no fear.

Laird no longer questioned the man as he caught the sense of urgency in the man, and ran after him, following along in a lumbering gait in his attempt to keep up with the black-clad warrior who seemed to glide across the floor. They both moved quickly down the long corridor leading to the space shuttle.

In the large room, Cubal was watching Blythe with a strange, curious stare. He'd just witnessed and experienced something that he could not understand. He'd known Blythe for many years. But, this was a side of the man he'd never seen nor sensed. Questions began to leap to his mind. He knew what he'd seen. He knew Butre did not fear any man.

*Butre feared Blythe.* The thought was stunning. He understood Butre, and knew the disciplines he and others like him undertook as children in order to totally control their fear levels. A Wearer of the Black took the ordinary, natural fear that came to a man and channeled it so that instead of generating a flood of fear, it merely sent the warrior into a state of alertness. Fear was something almost impossible for a Wearer of the Black.

Cubal had no doubt that both men were running for the space shuttle to take him and Laird to their ship. It brought back memories of the Crs'tings and their strange and sudden departure. They had been filled with such a fear, too.

"Who are you, Blythe?"

Blythe smiled and said, "I am Blythe. You know me, Cubal."

Cubal returned the smile and said, "No, I do not know you. I thought I knew you. However, I have just witnessed something that every bit of my training and experience tells me could not occur. But, it did. And so, my question to you is, who are you?"

Blythe nodded and said, "Come with me and we will talk. It is time for you to learn some things." He paused, then added, "Do not worry about Jules and Antal. They are safe." The man turned and walked briskly toward the room Laird and Butre had just vacated. Cubal followed silently.

Once inside the room, Blythe moved over to a large table and sat down. He motioned for Cubal to sit.

"Friend, there are questions in your mind, and I will answer many of those questions for you. Some answers will not come now, but will be answered in time. It is not for you to know everything, yet. But, one day you shall." He paused for a long moment, staring at his friend, then added softly, "What I will tell you must remain with you. It cannot be told to another, for now. Will you give me your word on that?

Cubal shifted his weight to balance his body and said softly, "Of course. You have my word." He stared hard at Blythe, then asked, "I did not really rescue you from the A'rkji did I?"

"Oh, but you did. Yes, you did."

"But was my intervention necessary?"

Blythe was silent for a long minute, then replied. "Yes, it was necessary that you rescue me. No, I would not have been slain if you had not intervened."

"But Blythe, I saw you beaten with the Berl whips and unconscious. "And, I have not detected in you any of the warrior signs, nor any of the energies that would signal me that you were anything but what you seemed to be."

He paused, then added, his eyebrows furrowed, "Until a short time ago, that is." He frowned, then continued, the frustration clear in his voice, "And even now, I do not detect anything in you except a peace and docility that would suggest you are the most vulnerable person on the planet." Cubal smiled and added, "We both know that is not true."

Blythe laughed softly. Clearly, he was enjoying this moment. He said, "Cubal, remember the times when I would speak to you of the Messiah, the one who ruled Earth for a thousand years?"

Cubal sighed, irritation evident in his voice. "Yes, I recall you speaking of the mythical god."

Blythe took no offense. "Well, I worked for Messiah on Earth for those years. And, before that, I was a soldier on Earth, but I was not slain in combat. I was executed with my family because of our belief and stand for Christ, the Messiah."

Cubal studied his friend for several minutes. Neither man spoke. Finally, Cubal said, "You ask me to believe that you have returned to life after being slain. It is a difficult thing to ask of another, you realize?"

"I know. And, I do not expect you to believe me, yet. My mere assertion of the thing is not proof of anything to you, except perhaps that I am delusional." Blythe smiled at Cubal and said, "I realize that all of your training and survival instincts are fully engaged, for you are re-evaluating me even as we speak, sorting out hundreds of scenarios in your mind, of things you might do in each of them. You have an incredible mind, Cubal."

The astonishment on Cubal's face was apparent. He said, "I will not ask how you know what you just said, for I have perfected the art of shielding my thoughts from others. There are beings who are able to draw the thoughts of a man from his head, and we trained against such enemies. But, it is clear to me that I did not train hard enough, or I am losing my ability."

Blythe laughed. "You are not losing your abilities. Indeed, you are gaining. But, you do not realize who, or rather I should say, *what*, I am. You see, I am what is known by some as a resurrected being, a human from the planet Earth who died and who rose again when summoned to life by Jesus the Christ, the Messiah, our King, our God."

Cubal actually felt the power of the man's feelings, the reverence that drove his words deep into Cubal's mind. He was careful as he spoke, not wanting to offend his friend, but not wanting to leave any false hopes. He replied, his words coming slowly, "I do not know what or who you are. I know you are a being called Blythe. I know what you have told me, but I am unprepared to accept such a thing since it is not something I have ever seen or experienced. Those who die are never seen again. It is only those who appeared to have died who are seen again. I have done such a thing on at least nine occasions."

"Cubal, it is not my place at this time to convince you of these things. My job at this time is to direct you, to give you some guidance and training, and to give you some things you will need. There are some who seek you, and their designs for you are evil. They would take your powers and use them to destroy the good, and to assist in an evil purpose. We cannot permit that."

"Who seeks me?" Cubal was intently curious, wondering if he would verify what he'd already been told. He did not know who these Ancient Ones were, and perhaps Blythe could explain more to him

"The one in Na'ha sought you, but he was only a hireling. He had been hired to deliver you to others. It was his device in the sky above us." He paused and smiled, understanding that his knowledge of the existence of the device would be significant to Cubal. Only a warrior trained in the art of D'vru would have detected such a device as it blended so perfectly with the sky above them.

He continued, "There are those who seek you in order to use your skills of war. They are called The Ancient Ones, and although they are very old and have lived on Earth many thousands of years, they are not human, but are beings created by one called Satan, or to some, known as Lucifer."

"Where might I find these ancient ones on Earth?" Cubal's voice was innocently curious.

Blythe smiled. "They will find you. Indeed, they already have. They know you are here. But, you will go to them, willingly. I know you have already made that decision. However, before you go, it is essential that we speak with you and give you three warnings, three pieces of knowledge, three gifts, and three training sessions."

"You say we. Who are the others besides yourself?"

"My father and my sister, and others you have never met. They will assist."

Cubal stood. "Let's be on with it then for I am anxious to meet these ancient ones who seek to use me."

Blythe smiled knowingly. He understood the complete absence of fear in the warrior, and of his desire to face those who sought him.

He also realized that Cubal, although a warrior without peer, was in great danger from these Ancient Ones. They and their leader was a far greater danger than the warrior had ever faced.

But, he would come to know that soon.

# Chapter 7

*"There is a force of the mind, and of the will, and of the spirit, and of the flesh. United and focused, the power of these forces is incalculable." D'VRU, BOOK TWO: The Force of Life (The Unity)*

Cubal slept for nearly three hours, unusual for him. When he awakened, he was alert and refreshed. A soft knock sounded at his door and he said, "Enter."

A lithe young woman entered with a tray filled with fruit. "Eat. You need to replenish your energies for the days to come."

Cubal smiled at her. "Carlith, it is good to see you once more. You do not appear to have aged." The words were spoken sincerely, and it was a matter of keen interest to him. She was at the age where she should be taller by now. There were no signs of her having aged.

"Oh, I am older and wiser, but alas, not taller."

"And are you also one risen from the dead?"

The question came suddenly, impulsively, and immediately he regretted having asked the question.

A faint smile curled the edge of one corner of her mouth as she replied, "You are not one to beat around the bush, are you?"

"Beat around...I don't understand your meaning, Carlith."

She laughed this time. "A saying, Cubal. Just an ancient saying. But, to answer your question, yes I am. I was slain with my brother, father, and mother, during the terrible persecutions we called The Great Tribulation."

"And, you also were a ruler on Earth during the one thousand years of this Messiah person?"

"I was there working, doing many jobs."

Cubal reached for a piece of fruit and asked, "So, when your king was removed from his throne, I take it you hopped on a vessel and fled with everyone else?"

She actually laughed, and Cubal found it an interesting and delightful sound. "First of all, Messiah was not removed. We stayed on there in the great city where His government was established. And afterwards, many of us were disbursed to various worlds to do many jobs. You happen to be our assignment at the moment."

Cubal chewed thoughtfully on a small piece of Kana fruit, enjoying its spicy aroma and its sharp flavor. Finally he looked at her and said, "And what is your assignment with me, exactly?"

Carlith tilted her head, thought for a long moment, then said, "I'm not able to tell you all of it other than I know that you are very important to God, and that there is a special task for you to perform for the Lord."

"Why does your God need me? Why not do it himself?" Although there was no smile on his face, there was a twinkle in his eye, and a small grin from one corner of his mouth.

She smiled. "That's a very good question. I used to wonder that myself until one day I discovered someone who needed help desperately, and I was able to give that help. It was such a satisfying experience for me, to know that I was needed, to know that I was able to help others, and to know that I am actually a servant of the Most High God. To serve God is the most satisfying feeling you can ever have. I know that I am an extension of Messiah, that my God actually works through me."

Cubal felt in her, as in Blythe, the power of her reverence. He said softly, "So you think that your God satisfies this need to serve by permitting you to be his servant?"

"Perceptive, Cubal, but not quite on the mark."

69

"The mark? What is mark?"

Carlith laughed again and said, "Not important. It is not merely God satisfying my need, but it is God *permitting* me to serve. It is a joy to serve God. I get to accomplish some great things for God and do things in the name of my Lord." She stared for a long moment at Cubal and said softly, "God does not need me to do anything. He could do anything he wanted without me. That's the incredible thing. He has chosen to work through such persons as myself, and Blythe, and my father, and my mother, and many others like us."

She paused for a long moment, smiled and added, "Even you."

Cubal took another bite of the fruit and munched slowly, digesting not just the food, but the words. That she was sincere, there was little doubt. She truly believed the things she said. But, he had met religious zealots of every kind and shape. She echoed similar sentiments and words he'd heard before.

But, he did have to admit that there was something different here. He wasn't sure what it was, but there was a difference. It was subtle, and went directly to his ability to sense things in people, including animals. He was a senser of life forces. And, with this woman, as with Blythe, the force of their life radiated brilliantly from them.

It was what had drawn him to Blythe in the first place. He'd never sensed danger nor killing power in either of them, but instead, a powerful, radiating life force that was different and stronger than any being he'd ever encountered. He'd always taken it to be a peculiarity of the race, though he'd not detected the same force in all individuals on the planet.

However, Cubal had visited too many strange places and seen too many strange sights to dwell on such things. He accepted what he found, and moved on, cataloging his new find, his new knowledge, and moving on to the next discovery. This had been merely another interesting piece of knowledge for him. And now, he at least knew that these people did have a power of some sort that was not obvious, and was, in some ways, greater than his own. They might worship a god of some sort, and perhaps this god gave them their power, but Cubal, Wearer of the Black, bowed before no god and served no master. He was a free warrior, and it would be so until the day he died.

He gazed thoughtfully at Carlith and said, "I'm certain that your god wishes to use me. That is apparent, for Blythe lured me here. This is nothing new. I have been used by many different leaders and kings and generals." He paused, and with a smile, added, "But, I confess I have never been sought by a god."

Carlith returned the smile. "*The* God, Cubal, not a god. Our God is the only God. The great I AM of the universe seeks you and your service."

"Well, he has managed to find me. I confess to being rather surprised that it took him so long to locate me, though." His voice held no sense of mockery, but again, the twinkle came to his eyes and a slight tilt to his lips reveal the beginnings of a grin. It was obvious that he was enjoying himself.

"You are a very likeable person, Cubal. I would enjoy conversing with you at length, but I cannot." Carlith ended the conversation by turning and exiting the room, the slight smile still on her lips.

The next three days were long periods of idleness. He did not inquire after his friends. Cubal knew they'd be taken care of and were probably enjoying the sights of the planet. He was as refreshed as he'd ever been, and the fruits had been exactly what he needed to re-balance his system.

*They'd known this.*

The thought whipped through his mind like the flash of a Carbian meteor across the skies. He did not try to follow the thought but concluded that somehow, these people were able to attune their minds to another's mind and body, and sense the needs there. It was a skill he'd seen long ago, and was one he had to a lesser degree. But, his was a shielded mind and body. He shielded his aura. It was a way of life for him, because an enemy can detect the entry points to one's being and discover vulnerabilities. But somehow, they'd still known.

*How can they penetrate my mind? What is their secret?*

It bothered him. He felt vulnerable, somehow.

On the third day, he was taken to a large, flat piece of ground. Blythe was there with his father. Cubal had not seen him for many years, and the man, like his children, did not seem to have aged. He strode forward and gripped Cubal in the hand. Cubal understood the ancient custom, and permitted his hand to be held by the other and

71

moved up and down. Blythe had introduced the handshake to him on their very first meeting many years ago. He did not understand it, but accepted it as their way of greeting. It was a custom followed by many humans he'd met through the years.

As though reading his mind, Nathan said, "In the ancient history of Earth, a warrior, to show you his friendship, and as a sign of peace, would stretch forth his right hand, the hand that clasped his sword, and by doing so, showed a hand empty of weapon. It was his way of offering no defense, and offering friendship instead."

Cubal's eyes widened as understanding came, and he smiled. "I like that. I had thought it to be a somewhat silly custom, but I see it now. It is a custom I shall adopt hereafter. It suits me well."

"Just beware of grasping the hand of an enemy who is holding his weapon in the other hand." Nathan was smiling.

For the first time in a long, long time, Cubal laughed out loud, his laugh deep and from the belly. He said, "You are not what you seem, Nathan. Between you and Blythe, I keep finding myself surprised." He paused, then added, "I suppose you are one of those resurrected beings as well?"

Nathan smiled. "Yes. We all died on the same day."

"Then, you are really his father?"

"Oh yes. He was my son. And, although we really do not have such roles now, we adopt them for convention's sake now and then. We enjoy it."

Cubal nodded his understanding, though there was very little of it he understood.

"You must receive your first three warnings. It is time."

Cubal smiled and said, "Begin. I am listening."

Nathan returned the smile and said, "Oh, these are not mere verbal warnings. These are warnings that you must absorb, must study, and must assimilate."

Cubal was silent, and when the other turned to leave, he began to follow. Nathan stopped and held the palm of his hand up. "You must stay here until you have taken in the warnings. You will know when it is time to leave."

Cubal stopped, then moved back toward a small tree. The others disappeared from view. Cubal waited, wondering what he was to do.

Nothing happened. For the next several hours he waited, but nothing happened. An ordinary man would have tired of the wait and simply walked away. Cubal had waited often in his life, and it had saved his life, this patience of his. Many times, it was the first to move who died, the first to betray his life force, who became victim. Waiting was easy for Cubal. And so, sitting lotus-like, he waited. The third day, he received the first warning. It was unexpected in its arrival and simplistic in its message, but there was no mistaking its meaning.

A small cloud appeared on the horizon and moved his way. It moved not with the wind, but contrary to its life. Cubal stood, sensing danger in the cloud, and alerted by the strangeness of its movements and by its presence in an otherwise cloudless sky. The cloud stopped above him, and instantly, Cubal moved to one side. As he moved, the cloud burst, leaking its contents on the ground below. A sizzling sound came and he observed the dirt and grass as it dissolved under the rain. And then it was gone.

The first lesson, he knew, was to beware of things appearing natural, but which are something else, and which moves contrary to nature. Such things may be deadly. Inside, they contain death. It was a lesson he'd learned long ago. Now, it was more than a lesson. It was a particular warning. He surmised that he was going to meet something that appeared to be natural, but would instead, be deadly.

The second warning came on the heels of the first. From near the base of a small hill came a man riding an animal. They appeared to be moving toward him. Cubal waited, his senses alert. As they approached, he recognized the man as Blythe. The rider slid from his mount and bounded toward Cubal. He moved to meet Blythe, then something from within Cubal stopped him. He never questioned these instincts, these deep, inner warnings. He was curious at Blythe's arrival here, but something from deep within kept him still. In seconds, he understood why, for before his eyes, the Earth opened, and the place where he'd have been was now an open wound in the ground, devouring all who dared stand or walk in that place. Instantly, the ground closed and Blythe disappeared.

He wondered at the second warning.

*I must not trust those who appear to be my friend?*

He decided that he was being warned that he could not trust his visual senses, and that no matter *who* he saw, he could not be sure they were really there, and that their images could be used to draw him into a trap. This too, was something that as a warrior, he had come to know. It was a tenet of D'vru. He wondered why they would give him a warning that was such a deep part of his training.

The third warning came within three hours of the first. It came in the form of an old man who walked up to Cubal and said, "You are the one chosen. It is upon your shoulders that the universe shall ride, and upon you shall all worlds come to naught. Your name shall be known by all and all shall come to your throne to pay homage."

Then, the old man smiled and held out his hand in order to shake Cubal's hand. The warrior was hesitant. The old man was insistent, his warm smile infectious. Cubal took the old man's right hand in his right hand and they shook. Suddenly, with a speed that could not have come from someone of such age, the man slapped Cubal across the face twice. Instantly, he disappeared before Cubal could even react, something that he'd have declared impossible seconds ago.

It did not seem possible that someone could have moved fast enough to have hit him, and even more, to have vanished before he could even strike a blow in defense. He'd never been hit in such fashion, and his cheeks burned with the sting of the slaps. He was not angry, because he understood there was no malice behind the blows, but instead, they were part of the warning. Cubal was unsure of the meaning of this third warning.

*Am I to Beware of old, white-haired men?* He smiled as the thought crossed his mind.

After a few minutes of thought, he dismissed it from his mind. He knew that at some level deep down within himself, he would be dwelling on this problem. However, it had been unsettling to him, having any man, particularly an old man, able to move fast enough to strike a Wearer of the Black. Such a thing had not happened to him since he was a young man learning the art of warfare.

Suddenly, Blythe and Nathan appeared beside him. He was startled, and whirled around, his defensive maneuvers making the wind swirl around all of them.

"I told you this was not a good way to come upon him, father."

Nathan laughed. "I know. But, I wanted to see what he would do."

Cubal had moved away from them instantly, and now he relaxed and moved back toward them. "I do not know how you do this magic, but I do not like it. Please do not startle me like that again. I may hurt you." He knew they had not merely shifted, as he could do. What they did was extraordinary. A shifter would materialize, but the appearance was not instantaneous to the trained eye. It was as though one were stepping out of a doorway, with the front parts visible first, followed by the rest. But, with Nathan and Blythe, their appearance was instantaneous.

Nathan said, "Cubal, you have been told some things about us that you do not believe. It is important that we demonstrate something to you. Please stand still for a moment."

Blythe stepped forward and stood before Cubal. "I know that you would not strike me, Cubal, but I also know that you are a warrior trained to survive. Therefore, defend yourself!"

The words were shouted, and as he spoke, Blythe struck at Cubal with a deadly beam of light. It sliced through the air at Cubal. But, the warrior was moving even before the light had begun its curve to his body, his hands invisible weapons cutting through the air. His blows struck Blythe less than a millisecond into the attack with a deadly effectiveness, and the weapon went flying. Blythe fell to the ground.

And immediately, he sprang up, unharmed.

Cubal stood at the ready, several feet distant, eyeing both men. He looked at Blythe in disbelief. He knew what he'd done, and knew there was no man who could have survived the deadly force he'd applied. It had been an instinctive move without conscious thought, reacting to a deadly force with a deadlier force. And yet, the man he'd slain was standing there unharmed. His skull should have been crushed. It was not.

Blythe said softly, "Cubal, it is not with pleasure that we did this, but we knew there was no other way to get you to attack one of us in order to demonstrate something to you."

Cubal's voice was low and measured, holding a tinge of anger. "I am unsure of what you have proven to me, Blythe. I know that I struck you. I felt the blow, felt your presence, felt everything. I felt your life force, measured it. And, I know that there is no human, and few alien species in the universe that could have taken the blows I gave you and lived. Yet, somehow, you live." He paused and stared at Blythe, a frown beginning on his face. "What have you proven, friend?"

"That we are immortal."

Cubal did not respond. It was a difficult concept to accept. He'd heard of immortals, but those had been stories. He'd never believed in them. Yet the proof was here. He'd seen it.

"You mean that you cannot die?"

Both men nodded. "We have tasted of death once. But, we are not merely resurrected beings. There is now no death for us, ever. We cannot die for our Lord is our life, and God cannot die. He is our life. In order for us to die, you'd have to kill God. That is impossible."

Cubal closed his eyes for a long moment, opened them, and slowly wiped a hand across his forehead and eyes. "The universe is a stranger place than I imagined. Immortals were always tales told, legends from the stars. But, just that. Until now, that is. There must be an explanation. It does not make sense to me."

He folded his arms across his chest and studied the two men in silence for a long time. "Both of you are strange beings. I do not have the answers concerning what you are, but one day I shall understand. I still cannot accept your god ideas, though."

Blythe stepped closer to Cubal and said, "My friend, you are a unique individual, more special that you could possibly know. And our King has a mission for you. It is for this purpose that you were born."

Cubal smiled. "Almost, I believe you."

"It is because you want to believe me. All humanity desires to believe that he or she exists for a purpose besides death." Nathan's voice was deep and resonant and full of authority. The big man stepped forward and placed his hand on Cubal's shoulder, then began walking him back to the large building housing the government of the planet.

As they walked, he began talking. "Cubal, there are three specific pieces of information that you are permitted to have. Our God has given us permission for you to know these things. The first is that the

Crs'tings were driven from Earth and the other worlds by our Lord and his angels."

Cubal's voice did not reveal the excited interest he felt. "And how did he do this?"

"I do not have the permission to tell this to you. What I was to tell you was explicit. I dare not go beyond." The man did not wait for Cubal to ask any other questions but continued: "The second piece of knowledge that you are to be given is that you did not come from the De'lith Laboratory Group. You were told that, and have believed that you came from that same group of DNA engineered warriors. But that is not your origin."

Cubal nodded and replied matter-of-factly: "I suspected that for a long time. Something in me told me it was not so."

"When did you suspect it?"

"During my training, within the first thirty years or so. When I would be around the others, there was a difference in us that I detected which should not have been if I'd been one of them."

Nathan grunted. "Good. You are very sensitive to your surroundings. That is excellent."

"Then, where did I come from?"

Nathan smiled. "Again, I am not permitted to tell this to you. But it is something you will learn in time." The man moved on without permitting further questions on the subject.

"The third thing that you are to know is that there is coming a terrible time of war in the heavens, and on the Earth. "Already, wars have begun. You had a part in the early wars. Indeed, you and others like you thought the time of wars ended. But, that was only a lull—an illusion. The peace that came was a false peace, and as you've seen on many worlds, there is no peace. Evil Slavers come and go at will upon the worlds, and men such as Laird continue their efforts to conquer and destroy."

Nathan stopped, and his voice changed, the tone lowering to one with a sense of foreboding. "The coming war will be different. Entire worlds will be completely destroyed and change shall come upon all the universe in the cleansing time. You will be a part of that time of war, but you must be prepared for it."

He resumed walking. "One of those groups who will enter the war against our God is the Crs'tings. They are more deadly now than before because they have invented weapons that did not exist when they first warred with us, and they have perfected certain techniques. They now have other allies who are very powerful. In the beginning, they shall prevail, and many shall perish. You will be the principle one to stand against them. But, it is not without danger to yourself for you may also perish in the war with them."

Cubal laughed, and with a touch of sarcasm in his tone, quipped, "So your god wants to use me, but is unable to protect me in my war against his enemies?"

"Oh, God is well able to do that, my friend. But, God's ways are so far above knowing, and his plans so intricate, there is no possible way we can understand all of them. Some die and some live, and it is all by his will. If our God wills that one live, then that one shall live, and if our God wills that one shall die, then that one shall die. He has not shared with us your fate, so we must presume that you may die in this war. Many others shall perish."

"Why then does he not simply will the death of all of the Crs'tings and those who oppose him?"

"He has already done that. Our Lord shall defeat all enemies, in time. But, there must first occurr certain things. His plan is above knowing, for it encompasses billions of lives, circumstances, and events, that must occur, all with precise timing, and in the order in which he has declared from the beginning. The mystery of iniquity must continue for a time in order to accomplish his purposes."

Cubal walked in silence beside the two other men, and as they entered the building, he stopped and said, "Nathan, I almost accept that you and Blythe are immortal. I confess to wondering whether I was deceived somehow, that I did battle with a vision. But, I think not. I do accept that you have strange powers beyond my experience. I accept that you can know things beyond the knowledge of any other beings I have met. But, while I accept that you work for someone called Christ, or Messiah, whom you call God, I do not believe this to be a god who created the universe and all that is in it. I cannot accept that your god was somehow slain and hung on a piece of wood, and later rose from a real death, and thousands of years later, was the same man who ruled Earth those many years."

He looked away for a brief moment, clearly uncomfortable with having to be so direct with his friend, but wanting him to understand his position and his reasoning. He continued, "Gods are not hung on pieces of wood, and mocked, and made a spectacle to their enemies. So, please understand, and do not be offended at my unbelief. I simply see you and those like yourself as another kind of being, even though you are unique beings. I acknowledge that you and your father are superior beings who are different from any others I've ever known. I also believe I must learn more about you and your kind."

"In order to survive, in the event you ever have to war against us?" Nathan folded his arms and stood staring at the warrior, a slight smile on his face.

Cubal's astonishment was visible on his face. And, just as quickly, it was gone. He said, "I forgot your incredible power of the reading of one's mind."

"I did not read your mind, Cubal. I was told by my Lord what you left unsaid."

"Perhaps. It is unimportant to me whether some creature you call god speaks my thoughts to you, or whether you view them inside me. The results are that you can know my thoughts. That disturbs me greatly."

"When you know God as I know God, you will understand how nothing can be hid from Him. He knows all, sees all, and is everywhere. He is that mysterious element long sought by Earth's astronomers and those learned in physics. His presence fills the universe and provides unification to it all, even to compelling the stars to maintain their place where there should be no gravity to make them obey."

Cubal's eyebrows raised, and he resisted the urge to grin his disbelief, but instead merely shrugged and said, "Well, let's get on with this. I believe there are more things that must be done. I am anxious to be on my journey and find those who seek me."

Nathan said, "It is good that you are anxious, for there is little time to waste. First, we must go to the Hall of Gifts."

After a short walk, they stepped through a huge, glimmering door that was shielded by some kind of special force field. Cubal felt the power of the shield, and it was stronger than those aboard the largest of a Gal-attack Spacial Ship. Cubal was ushered through the shield, and he marveled at the fact that the shield did not come down to permit his entry, yet there was not even a tingling of his skin.

Inside, on a huge, raised platform made of what appeared to be polished gold, there was a single seat. Cubal was escorted to the seat and commanded to be seated. He sat, and immediately felt power in the seat, a radiant, enveloping power that gave him great comfort and a peaceful tranquil feeling that he'd never known in his life. Suddenly, in the center of the platform, arising seemingly through the golden flooring as a spirit, rose what at first appeared to be a man, but was a kind of rack. On the rack was a hooded mantle of shimmering gold, more radiant that any he'd ever seen. Its folds rippled as though life filled the cloak.

Nathan said to Cubal: "Rise, and take the mantle, Cubal. It is a gift to you. You must first remove your old cloak for, from henceforth, this will be your cloak. It has associated itself with your cellular structure."

Cubal rose and shrugged out of his black cloak, which fell softly to the polished floor. He stepped near the mantle, took it from its place and laid it upon his shoulders and back, reaching to clasp the front with the strange buckle, which ignored his fumblings, for it seemed to find its place instantly, latching itself securely. As the mantle settled upon him, Cubal began to feel things within his body, and sensed a power in the cloak that seemed to radiate through his entire being. He stroked it gently, enjoying the supple softness of the strange cloth.

"What is the purpose of this strange cloak?" he asked.

"You will be told some of its uses."

Immediately, there arose from the floor in the exact center a cylinder, transparent and shiny, like polished, translucent silver. Inside, there was a small cushion, and upon the cushion what appeared to be another cylinder, a duplicate of the other, but much smaller, and with a strange golden glow to it. A door opened in the larger cylinder.

Nathan said, "Take the small cylinder, Cubal, and place it upon your belt. It's value will be revealed to you later."

He took the object and immediately the larger cylinder closed itself and disappeared. He waited for another appearance, but nothing came. Finally, he turned to Nathan and said, "I thought there were three gifts."

"There are. But, the third gift is not so visible. It will not be given at this time. It will come later, for there are conditions for this gift that must be met before you possess it. It is a gift that is greater than the other two gifts combined."

"What are the conditions for this gift? If I know them, then I can begin to work on them. What is the gift?"

"You will know when it comes."

"Is it immortality?"

Nathan smiled but was silent.

He stared beyond Nathan for a long moment, then shifted his gaze at the other and said softly, "Not even for immortality would I bend the knee, Nathan."

Nathan did not respond, but merely smiled his understanding at Cubal. Silently, the two left the room, and Cubal retired for the night. He munched on his fruit dish long into the night, staring at the landscape through his open window, thinking about the things he'd heard. He toyed with the golden mantle, feeling its suppleness, removing it, then trying it back on again to experience the feeling of warmth and peace it gave him, as well as the feeling of power that flowed through his body. The cylinder was something different. He pressed it, pushed it, rolled it on the floor, tossed it, examined it closely, smelled it, and even shook it near his ear. It did nothing. It seemed to be exactly as it appeared—a solid cylinder.

But he knew it was more. These were not the kind of people who gave useless gifts.

# Chapter 8

*"The eyes are an extension of the senses which are the most capable of destroying one's defenses." D'VRU, BOOK THREE: The Mind*

Cubal was called to a shielded room unlike any he'd ever seen before. It seemed to have no ceiling, yet he knew one was there. He suspected it was the same shield he'd stepped through in the Gifting Room, as he'd named it. This room was circular, had mirrors here and there, and three doors, each a different color. Beside the doors were statutes of what appeared to be a kind of ancient warrior, holding weapons of antiquity. One held a sword, another a spear and a third held an axe. Cubal was directed to the center of the room.

"You shall receive important instructions and training that are essential to your being able to stay alive in the coming conflict. Learn well, for if you forget, or if you ignore your training, you will surely perish, and it will not be a kind death, nor will your death necessarily be an instant one." Blythe was no longer the innocent looking boy-man he'd appeared to be so many years to Cubal. He was stern, and there was an almost military bearing about the man.

*This man has commanded troops.* The knowledge came to Cubal with sudden clarity and conviction. *He has been a warrior.*

"Cubal, remove the cloak and place it on the floor."

He removed the cloak and laid it at his feet and waited, alert, his training unwilling to permit him to relax for an instant.

Blythe stepped away from him and said, "There shall come upon you a cold unlike any you've ever experienced. Resist it as long as you can, and when you cannot resist any longer, quickly put the cloak upon your person, including the cowl."

The words were scarcely ended when Cubal felt a cold descend upon him that was beyond any cold he'd ever known. It was beyond the frigid, ice winds of Iclo, and even the waters on that barren planet had not contained this measure of cold. Cubal's body went instantly into survival mode. Trance-like, he melted to the floor beside the mantle and sat quietly, his mind retreating somewhere deep within himself, shutting down his body, regulating its temperature, closing his skin pores and raising the heat levels to compensate against the intense cold.

But, he who could sit naked in the snows of Chor'ta, and could sleep on an ice-flow on Iclo with warmth yet in his body, could not resist the penetrating cold that descended upon his body. He knew that no efforts he could make would combat this cold, and quickly, he reached for the golden cloak at his feet and threw it across his shoulders and covered his head with the cowl. Instantly, a warmth penetrated his being, flooding his senses with intense pleasure as it drove out the cold. He rose, a smile upon his features. He was genuinely pleased with this gift.

"Where does such cold live, friend?"

Blythe pointed up at the stars. "Out there. But, it can be created. Indeed, it has been created. There is a weapon even now being used on some planets to instantly freeze certain species. It does not work on humans, for they will perish. But, with some of the alien populations, when they awaken, they will find themselves on a slave planet, and will not recall how they got there."

Cubal's eyebrows furrowed. "There yet lurk beasts untamed in our space, I see."

Nathan stepped out from an invisible door and said, "More than that. There are beings out there whose evil is unspeakable, Cubal. That is why we are giving you weapons and training. These are things you must have if you will accomplish the task set forth for you to do."

"And what is that task?"

Nathan replied, "You will know in time. It is sufficient that you know that you will be fighting evil on a level never before known by mankind. But, you must be trained by us and others, and by trials above any you've ever experienced."

Then, Blythe stepped forward and said, "Now, remove your cloak again. This time, there will come upon you a great weight. Resist it until you cannot resist, then place the cloak upon your head and about your body."

Instantly, Cubal felt the crush of invisible weight. It was as though he'd stepped onto one of the giant moons of Ple'tha. But, the intensity of the weight kept increasing. Finally, he crumpled, and as he fell, he threw the cloak over his head and shoulders, snuggling beneath it as a child hides beneath its coverlets. The weight ceased. He stood, and there was no apparent weight upon him. He slowly removed the cloak from his head and immediately his head bowed and would have been driven to the floor but for his speed in re-covering his head.

He gasped, "What evil invented this weapon?"

Blythe waved his hand and said, "You may uncover your head now." He moved closer to Cubal and placed his hand on his shoulder, giving it an affectionate squeeze. "You are amazingly strong. You continue to surprise me. I would not have thought any creature could have stood as long as you did."

Nathan said, "This power is now being used as a mining tool. It was developed to crush entire asteroids into a small, condensed mass in space, then to tow it to a location for extraction. Unfortunately, the first time they used it, when they attempted to unpack the asteroid in order to extract its wealth, it exploded with the violence of an star going nova. It destroyed an entire world. But, they have modified it now, and although they still work with it in the hopes of using it as a mining tool, others have seen its potential as a weapon. They have reasoned that by increasing the gravity on a planet, they will be able to immobilize the entire population, including its armies. Once immobilized, they plan to invade through grav-free corridors and grav-free landing zones. Once the invading army is in place, the weapon will be turned off, and their army will move through the population, disarming everyone."

Cubal sighed. It was such a familiar sounding theme. Kill, murder helpless people, enslave populations and rule entire worlds. He'd fought against such evil once, years before, and thought it was over. But apparently, it was now worse than ever.

"From what worlds have these lords of war arisen?"

"From Earth, mostly. And, from your old enemy, the Crs'tings."

"Earth? Your home? The one where your Messiah ruled?"

"Yes. Once the Evil One was loosed, he busied himself corrupting the nations of Earth and sending his armies throughout the universe to destabilize and destroy. He knows that he has but a short time."

"A short time?"

Nathan hesitated, then said, "Lucifer was imprisoned for the years in which our Lord reigned. It was then that we learned to travel in space so efficiently, and discovered worlds, and found strange beings in these worlds."

Nathan folded his hands across his chest and continued, "Some of these alien creatures are not of God. And, some that are, have been corrupted by Lucifer. As he corrupted the Earth, he also has corrupted other worlds. He is the great destroyer. Eventually, he will be overcome and put in a place specially prepared for him and those who followed him. It is a place called hell by some. We call it The Place of Eternal Death, though some also call it The Place of Nothing. Carlith calls it The Fires of Eternity."

He pursed his lips and added, "That may be a better name, since it is a place where there is only emptiness—only disfigured spirits who are forever damned. There is a fire there unlike any kind of fire you would undestand."

Cubal was interested, and his curiosity showed on his face. "Tell me, why did your god loose him, if he had bound him? Why not just destroy this creature?"

"Our God does not reveal all things to us, but He shall one day. On the day of the Seventh Trumpet, we shall understand the mystery of evil. We know it was foreordained that Lucifer would be loosed. It was written in The Book long before our existence. We do not know why. We know that Lucifer is an indestructible being created by our Lord for his own purposes, and that there had to be a special place prepared for him that could contain him forever, for he has great powers. Of the angels, only Michael can withstand him unassisted."

"These angels were the mythical creatures associated with your beliefs, were they not?"

"Mythical, no. And yes, they are very much associated with our beliefs. But, they are very real. They are beings possessed of powers that exceed yours."

Cubal laughed. "Good. Let your god send them instead of me into this holy war of his and...."

Blythe interrupted. "Cubal, what you do not know is that the wars being fought are inter-dimensional wars. There is a spiritual war being fought all around you on many levels, for many things, and in many places. It is a war whose boundaries include the heavens. It is a constant war, and Michael is the chief angel in charge of these wars. God has assigned him legions for the battles, both on Earth, and now, in the universe on worlds you've never seen. A battle that is fought by Michael's angels on your behalf enables you to fight victorious in your battles, for without their intervention, you could not win. So, each time you are successful, realize that there were victories on another level, against unseen forces on your behalf."

For the first time, Cubal felt the flicker of doubt sweep through him. *I sensed them.* The thought raced through his mind like a raster beam through a hull.

His resistance to the notion that there was such a god as they espoused weakened slightly. He did not like knowing that he was giving the remotest of consideration to the idea of a god as described by his friend. But, he knew that he had often sensed the presence of unseen forces while in battle. He could not explain it, but he knew there was something, even as he'd known that something or someone had frightened the Crs'tings years before.

However, Cubal's mind would not permit him to remain long on a road to belief in an unknown, invisible god. He replied, his voice somewhat sarcastic, "Why does there need to be a battle in my world. Why can't this battle be waged on what you call your spiritual level?"

Nathan smiled and replied, his voice showing his amusement. "You are full of questions, Cubal. And, your ideas are sufficiently developed to keep you from seeing the truth. Suffice it to say that so long as there is a Lucifer walking the Earth, he will be attempting to kill you and every human in existence. He seeks the throne of God itself."

Blythe interjected, his voice somber. "Lucifer seeks to mount up to heaven itself and wage war in the midst of heaven." He paused for a long moment, then added, his voice low, as though he were speaking of something very secret and very disturbing: "But, he shall be defeated. Although he sends his emissaries into the heavens, and though he would storm heaven itself, he shall not prevail. Our Lord is able to speak, and at his word alone, the enemies of God will embrace death forever."

Cubal shifted his weight to one side, redistributing his energies, his warrior training ever present, even in a time of conversation with friends. He spoke softly, "I believe that it is possible that there is this evil person in existence. Indeed, I am convinced there are many like him. I even believe that there are beings who are invisible to me, for I have sensed their presence at times. I have felt the presence of great evil near me more than once, but I could see no person or being. And, it may be as you say, that this evil one seeks to wage his war to the very throne room of your god. I will accept what you say as truth. But, I still do not accept the concept of god, for there are no gods, only beings who are superior."

Blythe changed the subject abruptly and said, "You must learn more of the cloak, my friend, for there are other uses for it that you do not know." He turned and called out. A door opened and three men walked through the door. Each of them carried a weapon. One carried what appeared to be a sword, another a spear, and the third, an axe. They moved to the center of the room and stopped.

Blythe spoke to Cubal, his voice loud enough for all to hear. "These are warriors. They are not immortal, so do not harm them, Cubal. Whatever you do, you must not harm them."

"I seek them no harm."

Blythe smiled. "But, they will seek your harm."

"Then, I will seek their harm."

"No, you will not. You will do exactly as I've told you to do." The voice was a command, and he felt the force of it as the words impacted him. He stepped back, amazed that anyone could do that with his voice to him, a Wearer of the Black.

"Then I will defend."

"No, you will not defend yourself. You will place the cloak upon your person as you did with the gravity attack. You will not need the cowl this time. And, you will not flinch nor move as they attack."

Cubal took a deep breath. It was not his nature, nor in his training, to stand still while an enemy attacked him. But, he'd seen what the cloak had done already, and he trusted Blythe. The cloak had strange powers, and he knew he needed to explore its uses.

"I will remain still." He covered himself with the cloak. But the training within him took over, and even though he knew he would accept the blow, his body was prepared to resist its penetration.

The three, as one, advanced toward Cubal. One whipped his sword above his head and swept it down at Cubal's head. Incredibly, just a millisecond before Cubal would have moved aside, contrary to his promise, the weapon swerved and spun the wielder of the sword around with the force of the deflected blow.

The man with the axe hurled his axe straight at Cubal. He waited, knowing that he could move out of the way with ease, even at the last fraction of a second. The axe veered, as though deflected by an unseen hand, and the weapon clattered to the floor. Even as the sounds were echoing, the spear raced its way straight to the heart of the warrior. And, as happened to theother weapons, it also suddenly darted to one side, deflected by the power of the cloak.

Cubal was smiling now. "I like this cloak even more."

Blythe motioned for the three men to leave. After they'd left, he said, "Cubal, it will act as a deflector against all objects that are rock, metal, or any combination, glass, precious stones, and even wood and plants. It will not deflect laser or raster light, though it will absorb and partially deflect even that for a brief time, perhaps half a minute."

Cubal laughed. "In half a minute, a Wearer of the Black can slay twenty men."

"You no longer wear the black."

Cubal thought for a moment. "It is true. You have taken from me a cloak I wore most of my life and replaced it with one that shimmers its golden color about the room as a target."

Blythe laughed and said, "Ah, you are about to learn more of this cloak. I think you will like it even better." At that, the light in the room dimmed to a level which would illuminate the room if a full moon were shining through the open roof. Cubal discovered that his golden cloak was the exact duplicate of the darkness around him. He removed the cloak and found that even from a foot distance, he could not see the cloak. It was invisible.

"That is an incredible thing!" he exclaimed. "I would not have believed it if I did not see it with my eyes." He laughed out loud at his words.

Nathan came closer and took the cloak from his hands. The lights rose to full daylight. "Watch closely, my friend." He stepped away from Cubal nearly a dozen feet, then swiftly, he reversed the cloak, draped it about his head and shoulders, and crouched to the floor.

"Am I to believe that you hide beneath the cloak on the floor, and that I cannot see you, though I am looking exactly where you crouched, and though all my senses tell me you are there?" Cubal's voice was cracking with disbelief.

Suddenly, Blythe rose and removed the cloak. "It is as you said, friend. Reverse the cloak, and in the brightness of the sun, you will be hidden from all sight. Nothing can detect you except for certain animals, some beings whose senses are as trained as yours, and one particular sensor device that will notice an object in a location where an object should not exist. It will sound an alarm against you. Of course, even if the alarm is sounded, those who come to the alarm will not see you. Only, be sure to move in such instance, because they will be searching a specific coordinate, and if you've moved by the time they arrive, they will find nothing."

Blythe handed the cloak back to Cubal. The warrior put it upon his shoulders and said, "Are there other secrets to the cloak?"

"Others, yes, but none that you need to know of this day. The cloak is perfectly attuned to your body energies, and will only be energized by your touch. No other may use it unless the cloak is touching you."

Nathan stepped forward and said, "Give me the cylinder, Cubal."

He handed the man the small cylinder, and, as Cubal watched in astonishment, the man spoke to the cylinder a single word:

"Cover!" Immediately, Cubal saw a faint glow appear around Nathan and realized it was the same force field he'd seen in the first room which had covered the open ceiling in this room. But, this field had enveloped Nathan and followed the shape and contour of his body perfectly. He watched as the man walked, and the shield followed in perfect unison.

He then spoke another word: "Cease!" and the field disappeared. Then he spoke again: "Front!" and a field sprang into existence several feet in front of Nathan.

Nathan had the field collapse again, then spoke another word: "Above!" The field appeared above his head about ten feet, circular and nearly invisible. Nathan collapsed the field, then said: "Below!" and a field, again circular, appeared beneath his feet. He collapsed the field again, then handed the cylinder to Cubal.

"You have heard the commands. This device will only listen to your voice. It is set to your energies so that it will not harm you, and will recognize only your patterns of voice and mind and body energies."

"Why then did it obey you?" asked Cubal.

"I am not bound by such things for I became you for a brief time."

"Would it, or the cloak, obey a Crs'ting?"

Blythe laughed. "You are never still in your mind, are you my friend? Always calculating the odds, always measuring the enemy. Good! You encourage me greatly."

He rubbed his hands together in delight, then answered Cubal's question. "No. They lack one thing that you have which is essential for the operation of this device. They have no spirit. It is this which you've sensed lacking in them. They are created beings, spawned by the Evil One, created to wreak havoc in the universe and to depopulate and replace humans on the Earth, and from whatever planet they find them living. But, they cannot use this, even if one has cloned himself into a duplicate of yourself, as one did against you so long ago."

Cubal's eyebrows arched. "You know about that?"

Blythe smiled. "We watched the battle."

Cubal snorted his disbelief. "I have allowed much with you two. But this, I cannot accept. There were no others around. This I know, for briefly, I was at a level seven, a level I've only achieved once, and I would have sensed any living organism within a thousand meters. All around me was death and emptiness. I saw no other beings alive."

*But I did have the sense of being watched. Someone had watched the battle.* The memory of the battle flooded his mind.

"I assure you," replied Nathan, "he and I, and several others stood nearby and watched the battle." He paused for a long moment, studying the warrior, then added, "But, there was a battle prior to that which protected you and strengthened you."

Cubal's eyebrows raised. "I saw no other battles nor signs of battles just before that one. We stalked each other, and it was a silent battle on virgin soil that had never seen death before, for the grass was shining and bright with life."

"This was not a battle you would have seen, my friend. But, it was waged on your behalf, nonetheless."

"I assume by these god creatures you call angels?" There was no sarcasm in Cubal's tone, but the skepticism was evident in his eyes and on his face.

"Yes. They watched your battle with us."

Cubal laughed. "Tell me then, O watchers of my life, what did I do to avoid death from this creature?"

Instantly, Blythe replied. "You executed a maneuver to evade him that was from beyond your experience, thus something he could not have duplicated. You made your body do something that you'd never done before, never even thought of before, and was not part of your training. It was, in fact, contrary to your training, for in doing the maneuver, it exposed you to this creature for a brief fraction of time, and thus, it was not a maneuver you'd ever have been trained to use. But, because it was something unexpected, it was exactly the move to make, and it brought him into the trap and enabled you, ultimately, to defeat the Crs'ting in the seventeenth minute of the battle."

Nathan added, "You learned that you were just a bit faster than the Crs'ting. It was this knowledge that gave you the advantage you needed."

Cubal took a deep breath and said, "I don't know how to react to your statements. All you say is true, but I cannot be sure that you are reading my mind, or that you were in fact there."

91

Nathan smiled and was quiet.

Blythe laughed out loud, looked at Nathan and said, "Thomas must be loving this."

Cubal raised his eyebrows, expressing wonder at who Thomas was, but remained silent. He was busy thinking about what they'd said.

*They may have watched, after all. Someone did.*

"Well, let's go. We're finished here, Cubal." Nathan stepped toward the exit.

Cubal was led to his room.

The time for leaving was near.

# Chapter 9

*"The movements of death are recognized by those who understand the movements of life."   D'VRU, BOOK One: Movements of the Warrior, (The Beginning)*

Cubal knew they were coming for him. He'd stayed in his room for the rest of the day. But now, he was ready to leave. It was as if they knew he was ready. Cubal had worked many long hours perfecting his thoughts and movements with the cloak and the shield.  He'd practiced every conceivable scenario, recalling hundreds of battles and situations, duplicating them in his movements and adapting the shield or the cloak or both as appropriate, until he reached the point to where his use of them was natural and without conscious thought. There was no hesitation in any of his moves with the cloak. The cylinder he'd placed in a small pocket in the front of his wrap at his midriff.

Blythe escorted him through the complex. He was silent until they reached the edge of the spaceport. He stopped, turned to Cubal and said, "May God be your protector and give you grace, my friend."

Cubal smiled and extended his hand in the manner of the handshake which he'd adopted. As they shook hands, he asked, "To where do I go? Or, do I just decide that on my own?"

"You may go as you please. Perhaps you might want to go to Antal's home planet. He will learn there of his birth."

Cubal's eyebrows raised. "And would that be the planet Ex'tal?"

Blythe smiled and nodded his affirmation. "Cubal, the ones who seek you know where you are and only await your departure. They understand this is a protected planet."

"I take it you mean those called the Ancient Ones?"

"Yes."

Cubal stared beyond Blythe for a long moment, then replied, "I must tell you this about me. There is no fear within me of another being. I approach all beings with a respect for their life, until I discover differently. The Ancient Ones may not seek my life. They may seek me for good. I will learn why they seek me. They may not present for me the danger you think." A faint smile tilted one corner of his lips. "And, I assure you, I will one day know exactly why they seek me."

Blythe hesitated, then said, "Our God has revealed certain things to us, Cubal. I am permitted to tell you that they seek from you service and allegiance. I also know that you are trained from birth to act independently in your thought and your decisions, especially when it comes to tactics in battle. It is part of what makes you special. You are able to enlist in a cause independent of what others tell you, based solely on your own observations and conclusions. However, I hope you will not give your allegiance to them."

Cubal smiled. "As you said, I have given allegiance before to others in the past. Why not them, if I choose?"

Blythe returned the smile and folded his arms across his chest. "Life is a series of choices. Only the wise know to choose rightly. And, as your own teachings say: Let the warrior choose the battleground and it will be rugged terrain, for there, he may deflect energies and enlist the rocks to his cause; let him choose the enemy, and he will choose a foe worthy of his efforts; but let him choose the cause, and he will choose the cause of peace."

Cubal raised his eyebrows and his eyes narrowed as he studied this strange being he called friend. He looked at the ground for a long moment, turning over his thoughts in his mind before he spoke. Finally, he asked, "How is it that you know the D'vru writings?"

"We have known of them for many years. Their origins were on Earth."

"This I know, but I also know that they were very secret, and those who were taught were never to reveal them."

94

Blythe laughed. "There are no secrets from God, Cubal."

Cubal shook his head. "You keep speaking of this god as though he knows everything, yet he does not know whether or not I shall serve the Ancient Ones."

"Oh, but our God does know, Cubal. He does know the answer to that. I do not know, but God knows. We only know what God chooses to reveal to us." Blythe studied Cubal silently for a few moments, then with a slight grin on his face added, "I suspect you'd find service to the Ancient Ones very different than you suppose, since theirs is an evil service."

Cubal's face showed his disbelief. "I go with no purpose or intent except to learn why they seek me. Perhaps I shall serve them in order to show your god that he does not know what I shall do. Would that not prove your god's powers are not what you supposed them to be?"

Blythe nodded his head negatively. "You do not understand, my friend. But, it is not time. You must go the path that you will choose, and things must happen as they shall. However, know this, Cubal, Wearer of the Gold, our God also seeks your service. Indeed, He seeks far more than service. He seeks your absolute loyalty, and your worship."

Cubal frowned. "Loyalty is something I could give to another, perhaps even this creature you call god. But, worship is not something I can ever give to another being. Not even to one called a god."

Blythe smiled. "Your superior training has made you supreme in your mind, Cubal. I fear your pride may be your undoing one day."

"Pride? I do not understand. I know who I am and what I am. I understand my abilities. I do not boast of them, nor do I hold others in contempt who have not my training and abilities. How then do you say I am proud?" The clipped words came in a burst with a trace of anger.

Blythe held up his hand with a smile across his face. "Forgive me, friend. I do not mean to offend you."

Cubal shrugged and said, "It is nothing. But, one last question, Blythe. When you warned me not to transport myself through the web field, will you explain to me what would have occurred and why."

Blythe said, "Your ability, learned from Antal, is a very old technique which involves moving inter-dimensionally. Few humans have ever mastered it. This was taught to certain elite followers of the Evil One during the times of great wars on Earth, before Messiah's rule. At that time, there was great trouble, and his army needed to escape total destruction. This knowledge was passed on to others, and eventually, the secrets became known to a few on Earth, and to certain ones on the planet Ex'tal, where they trained many of their male children from birth in this technique, such that in time, some of the children seemed to instinctively pick up the technique with little or no training."

Blythe moved ahead just a few feet and pointed to a distant tree. "That tree is the limit to which you should move, for moving a greater distance than that can cause your death. Your body is not made to withstand the sudden shift of atoms and molecules. Over great distance, it can be deadly for you. The Ex'talanians learned this the hard way, for they lost many lives in the early days."

Cubal said, "This then is why Antal would not move very far. But, what of the force field? Is it a danger for me to shift through all force fields?"

"No. But, the one they were using is special. It was designed for persons who can shift. If you attempt to shift from the field, it will render you unconscious instantly, and can hurt you."

"So, how do I know when the field is one like that?"

"By its web-like features. It will never appear as a normal force field, but will always have the appearance of a web." He turned then and pointed to a small, oval vessel, milky white, with a sheen to its hull. "Your friends are already inside waiting."

They parted with a brief wave at the other, and Cubal quickly entered the small transport vessel. Jules was seated, inspecting his weapon. Antal was standing near a slitted window peering out.

"Friends, I trust you had a pleasant stay?"

Jules replied instantly, a tinge of irritation in his voice, "Pleasant, but boring. Where did they take you?"

Before Cubal could respond, Antal said, "What a magnificent cloak, Cubal." He reached out and stroked it gently. "Where is the dark cloak?"

Cubal smiled at his huge friend and said, "I no longer am a Wearer of the Black. I am Wearer of the Gold." He moved quickly to the controls of the vessel and said, "Now gain your seats. We must travel to another world." He looked back at Antal and added, "One that will be of interest to you especially, my friend. It is your home."

"Home? We return to Na'ha?"

"No. We go to a place called Ex'tan. It is your real home. You are not of Na'ha." Cubal laid his seat back to a reclining position and said, "Now rest," then closed his eyes.

In a short time, a small voice from the control panel sounded, its emotionless tonal patterns giving a pleasant alert to the voyagers. "You are now at destination. Signal has been confirmed to journey to planet, and all systems are locked on docking transition."

A gentle nudge followed soon after indicating the vessel had been cradled. A few minutes later, the trio stood in the Grasl Hall of Embarkation, famous throughout the worlds as the place where seventeen Ex'tanian warriors fought off an entire legion of raiders, consisting of a large contingent of A'rkji soldiers and a mixture of other beings. It helped that the Ex'tanian's had the assistance of Cubal.

*It is still there.* Cubal smiled as he saw the huge green splash on one entire wall. It was the green life force of the Endril'sta warrior whom Cubal had slain during the battle. It was this creature's death that turned the battle for them. The Endril'sta warrior was a formidable foe, an enemy larger than ten ordinary humans, towering over all others, and clad in natural shell that grew from its body, which acted as armor. He was a ferocious fighter, and had slain fifty defenders on landing. Cubal's small force of seventeen had met the invasion force in the Grasl Hall because if they'd passed that point, they would have access to the transport ways of the planet, and many thousands would have been slain before they could be stopped.

After holding off the force for a time, the Endril'sta warrior had challenged the small opposition force to a personal battle between just himself and the "dark warrior," as he'd called him. Cubal had accepted the invitation, and the battle had been fought in the large open floors of the Embarkation Hall. It had not been an easy battle, for this alien warrior had a resiliency even greater than the Bora tiger. He was supple and did not break, and his body absorbed blows that would have destroyed other creatures. Finally, realizing that he had to move quickly, Cubal had lured the huge creature over near the wall. Once there, he'd quickly snared the creature's feet in a Berl lasso and, running in a circular pattern, whirled the creature around and around, finally hurling him against the wall with such force that its shell shattered, and its life force impregnated the walls with its pale green blood.

"Is it really you, sir?" A tall man limped his way toward the trio. His attire was that of a soldier, with purple stripes running down each pants leg, his upper torso clad in the traditional red of the Ex'tanian Elite Guard. The single emblem of an ancient Earth clock face rested on one sleeve, indicating that he was of the High Order.

"Barcel! I had thought you to have retired and gone to live in the hills somewhere by now."

The man grasped Cubal by the shoulders and squeezed his affection. "I will never retire. I lost a leg seven ages ago, and it was then suggested I quit." He pulled up a pant leg and revealed a leg that was somewhat smaller than the other. "Our doctors did not do such a good job grafting as they do on Earth. The fool forgot to reinvigorate the new leg and reimpose the DNA structures properly. It shrank." He smiled, then added, without rancor, "So I limp." He looked quickly at Cubal's two companions, his gaze lingering on Antal for a long moment, then asked, "So, what brings you here, warrior?"

"I come here to get some questions answered for my friend here." He nodded at Antal. "Many years ago, he was brought to the planet Na'ha, in the jungles there. He was brought by people of the planet Glale. We have just left there. They did not give us any answers, but did confirm that Antal is of this planet. I know it to be true because he is a shifter. He has the gift."

Barcel peered intently at Antal. "I knew upon looking at him that he was of this planet. He is clearly one of us, though his size is somewhat larger than ourselves. In fact, I do not recall ever seeing any of our people quite so large."

"I believe his growth was altered because of his stay on Na'ha. The difference in gravity, the red sun, and the diet probably altered some patterns of growth in him."

Barcel smiled. "Indeed it must have." He was silent as he studied the big man longer and more closely. Finally, he said, "There is a look about him. He appears to be someone I know, but I do not perceive who it might be."

"Well, let us do what we must to find out." Cubal turned from his friend and began heading out of the Hall.

Barcel said, "We can journey there as in the old days, friend, which will take us an hour, or if you prefer, there is a transport vehicle over here." The man was pointing at a small transport used for the transfer of people and luggage. Cubal followed the man to the transport, anxious to continue his journey.

Within seconds, the four found themselves standing on a large balcony overlooking the city. It was a busy city, the largest on the planet, and Cubal could see that since he'd last visited, much had changed. Small vessels roamed the city, some marked with the blue and grey of the city police, others of many colors, obviously belonging to citizens moving about the city. The buildings were mostly built of a translucent material, though there were some still standing that were built in another era, made of rock and steel.

In a few minutes, a man approached them, and after a quick, whispered conversation between the man and Barcel, Antal and Jules left with the man. "I have sent Antal and your other friend to the Health Center where they will sample his DNA and molecular structure. We have a record of every birth on this planet. We will soon know of his origins." Barcel moved to a large, comfortable looking chair, and threw his withered leg onto the top of a small table.

"Good. In the meantime, tell me what you know of shifting." Cubal stood a few feet away facing the other.

Barcel blinked. He paused for a long moment and said, "It is forbidden. I cannot."

Suddenly, Cubal disappeared and reappeared behind Barcel.

"Are you sure you cannot speak with me?"

The startled soldier jerked his head around and saw Cubal standing there. He said softly, "I should not be surprised that one such as yourself has learned the technique. It is something sacred with us, Cubal. We teach it to those children whom we begin training to be warriors. But, there has been a movement of late to teach it to all our people. Some say it is something that could save many lives if ever there was an invasion and our wives and children needed to escape. The argument has merit. But, the military and the police argue against that because they feel that if it becomes a common thing, then all will know the secret, and it will be told to others, even enemies, and our secret will be no more."

He reached to the table and lifted a small glass of Trellian tea and sipped at the bitter-sweet drink. "I am of that opinion."

"I wish only to know your experiences in its uses. I need to know the limitations, for it is a technique that I will use from time to time."

The soldier wiped a hand across his grey hair and said, "I cannot speak with you of this, but I can speak to the Council of Five. They will hear the matter and decide whether we can share with you."

The two men talked for long hours into the setting of the sun. Antal and Jules returned later in the evening and they all discussed the events from when Antal was deposited on the planet Na'ha. Finally, Barcel departed, promising to return once he'd learned the Council's wishes.

In another day, Barcel had not returned, and Cubal became concerned that he was denied in his petition. He was weary of remaining in the spacious quarters Barcel had provided for them, and was anxious to be on his way to inquire of those who sought him. Although it might be some kind of mission to Blythe and Nathan, for him it was a personal matter. He would not sit by idly while others sought him. It was not his way.

He gathered his small pouch of belongings, put on the cloak and prepared to leave. "Antal, you will learn here the mystery of your beginnings. Jules, return to the jungles, or stay with Antal, as you choose. My friend will see to it that a vessel returns you home if you wish. I must leave. Oh yes, when you return, if you go near the place where Antal was discovered, there is a small valley there, and beside that valley, a great tree of white and gold. I have a small transport vehicle parked there. Keep it for me. Use it if you wish. I will retrieve it some day."

Jules stood quickly and walked over to Cubal. "I will find it and care for it. Journey well. It is good that we have known you. But, is it not possible that we can journey with you?"

Cubal stared long into his friend's eyes, then replied, his answer soft with regret: "No, Jules. To come with me could be to perish, for the journey I take may be dangerous, and if it is, then it would surely end in your deaths."

"I have grappled with death before."

Cubal smiled. "Indeed you have, and you shall again, I'm sure. But, not where I go."

Antal was silent, remaining seated. Finally, he rose slowly and approached Cubal. "I thank you for returning me to my home. But, I cannot remain here. I may have begun my journey here, but this is not home. If we do not continue with you, we will both return to Na'ha."

Cubal clasped the big man's hand in a shake and said, "It is good. You will be brothers there."

With that, he stepped out of the room, and moments later, had stepped through a transport and was headed for his vessel. Just as he was climbing into the vessel, he was hailed by a familiar voice: "Cubal! Wait!"

He turned to see Barcel limping toward him.

"I have the permission from the Council of Five. They will teach you whatever you want to know."

Cubal replied, "I cannot wait any longer, Barcel. It is urgent that I leave. But, tell me one thing about shifting. If I attempt to move, say, through a rock or a metal, say the hull of a ship, are there any dangers?"

Burcel chuckled. "You have an instinct for survival, don't you? If you shift yourself into a solid mass of anything, you will perish. If you shift beyond it, you are safe, excepting for any Berl clad object. Never shift through such material. You will survive, but you will suffer burns over much of your body." The man fell silent.

Cubal nodded. "And here's a caution to you that you must pass on to your people. There is a new kind of shield that will appear as a web. Do not attempt to shift through such a web, as it will harm you. It may not kill you, but it will harm you, at the least render you unconscious, and  perhaps even damage your brain."

"I will pass on that information. This is new to us. How did you learn this?"

"On the planet Glale. I was entrapped in such a web. Fortunately, I was warned in time to stop me from shifting."

The soldier resisted asking more questions. He was curious to know more, but did not press the matter. He knew the warrior was anxious to leave.

Burcel said, "Cubal, we have learned of Antal. His parents died while he was a child. They were in a space transport being used to bring mining supplies to a distant moon. We believe raiders attacked the vessel. We found the ship stripped, and all the crew and passengers dead. Antal and two other children were missing. Apparently, the raiders came from the planet Glale."

Cubal shook his head. "No, whoever raided the ship did not come from there. I know those people well, and I assure you, they did not do such a thing. They were able to save Antal, for it was they who deposited him on Na'ha. They are a very holy people who worship the one who ruled the Earth for so long. Whether he is a god or not, I do not know, nor care, but I do know they are a good and honorable people"

Burcel nodded his head. "We have had visits by them from time to time. They were a very soft-spoken people. If they are all as those were, I doubt there's a soul on the planet who would lift a finger against an invader. Indeed, it is puzzling that they have not been invaded and subdued in all this time."

Cubal stopped and turned to his friend. On his face was a slight grin. "Their appearances are not as they seem. It would be a serious error for anyone to mistake their apparent docility for an inability to defend themselves. This I know, for it was one of these docile souls who saved me from the web of a force field."

*"And they did it all with mere words.* The thought lay dormant, unuttered to his friend. It was a mystery beyond his comprehension.

"Well, that is something worth knowing. I must believe you, but I do not understand. That they are a religious people, I know, for they refused our Toca beverage which brings one to an enlightened state of mind. They said their god would not permit their taking such drink." Burcel stopped as they reached the vessel, and said, "Goodbye my friend. May we both live to fight another battle together."

"May it be so, Burcel. Take care of my friends."

Burcel stepped back into the shadows, then stopped and asked, "But, where is it that you go, my friend?"

Cubal's face was expressionless and his eyes looked beyond his friend as he answered: "Earth. I seek the Ancient Ones there."

# Chapter 10

*"The beginning of a move is the setting of the balance point for all that follows." D'VRU, BOOK ONE: Movements of the Warrior, (The Beginning)*

Cubal stepped into the vessel, and a moment later, it winked out of sight, sliding through the dimensional slipstream discovered by Chale, an Earth scientist during the time of the reign of the Christ king. Many inventions had come during those days, and space travel, thought possible before, became common, for there were no more limits on speed, and time was no longer a serious factor.

Although he was, in terms of light years, many millions of light years away from the planet known as Earth, he would enter the Earth atmosphere in just under twelve minutes of time. He had visited Earth once for just a short period near the end of the reign of the Christ king. He'd found Earth to be the most organized and well managed planet he'd ever visited. Its streets were free of debris of any sort, and lined with beautiful flowers, fauna and trees of every sort.

But, the thing that had impressed him most was the complete absence of soldiers and police. He was told there was virtually no crime there, and that the penalties for crime were severe. There was no tolerance for illegal actions on the planet. There had been no visible signs of any soldiers or other police forces usually required to maintain the peace, and to keep law and order.

It was also the most populated planet he'd ever visited. There were people in every part of the planet. Giant cities, unlike any in the galaxy, were in abundance on the planet. The several cities he'd visited were like huge gardens, with small paths throughout the entire city, each path taking one through a maze of gorgeous plants and flowers. Fruit trees were in abundance, and the fruit could be picked at will, although he'd seen what appeared to be workers who apparently tended to the picking of the fruit on the trees.

He'd studied much of the literature while there, and even went into the interior where there were no cities, and explored in some of the forests. Even there, he'd discovered people living. They'd all seemed to be a very happy and prosperous people. Not once had he found anyone seeking the life of another, nor the usual hawking of wares that he'd seen in most other cities.

He had seen some who disputed with one another over what appeared to be minor things, such as one man who felt his neighbor's plants were too large and were blocking the sun from his porch. Cubal had sat on a chair nearby in a kind of café, drinking a beverage of chilled water mingled with the juice of a purple fruit called grape, watching. They'd exchanged words, but there was never the threat of violence.

Now, it was different. Earth had changed. Immediately, he sensed the difference. There was the smell of death in the air, and he sensed hostilities all around him. The people did not have the same pleasant attitudes as before. There was a wariness that only comes from those who hunt or are hunted. And, there were soldiers now. Odors of decay hung in the air.

Three large soldiers, each one over seven feet tall and broad shouldered, approached him, weapons at the ready. The leader was a gruff-looking man with a huge, dark beard. He said, "Present yourself for identification, traveler."

Cubal stood still, evaluating the men. Though he sensed their readiness, he also realized that they were merely performing a perfunctory chore. He extended his left hand on which a small bracelet hung. "I am Cubal."

The man gave the bracelet a quick scan with his finger reader, then looked at a huge screen overhead. Cubal sensed the change in the man instantly. Something had startled the soldier. Cubal did not turn to look at the screen.

"You are expected, honored sir. Please follow us." The soldiers turned as one and began marching ahead.

Cubal followed along, one thought echoing in his mind: *How could they have been expecting me?*

They stepped onto a transport platform, and the bearded soldier said, "You will be sent to a small waiting room on the other side of the planet. Wait there until you are called."

They stepped back and watched as Cubal wrapped his cloak around himself and stepped into the portal. Whoever he was about to meet was very powerful. Cubal began the de-energizing of his mind, lowering his level of existence to that of an older, less powerful man. It had saved him from attack more than once, and caused his enemy to underestimate his powers. He did not know who he might meet on the other side of this transport, but he did not want them to be able to measure him properly. There were instruments that could measure a man's strength, and he was fairly certain these instruments would be employed here.

He stepped into a room dimly lit, with a faint musky odor akin to that of a room that has had moisture in it for a long period of time. It was a small room with chairs of an ancient design, resting against the walls. The building was very old, older than any building he'd ever been seen. High up near the ceiling were wooden beams across the tops. They were grey with time.

He walked slowly to one of the chairs and seated himself. *They know who I am. Who are they?* No doubt they were now discussing his arrival. Certainly, they were planning the meeting, measuring their approach carefully, in order to achieve their objective. He felt his pulse quicken with anticipation.

*What is it that makes me love the threat of danger?* It was an idle thought. He caught himself and began his focused, inward modeling of his mind and actions. He needed to be very reserved, very restrained, and had to rise to a higher level in order to shield his thoughts and energies.

Suddenly, the huge wooden door at the end of the room opened with a creak. A small man, clothed in a faded brown robe, walked slowly out of the room and stood beside the door. He had a large staff in one hand. The man rapped the staff on the floor hard three times, and in a loud voice, proclaimed: "My Lords, if it please thee! Cubal, Wearer of the Black seeks audience with thee!"

106

If Cubal had been on a different level of control, he would have been startled. But, he did not react, did not wonder, and instead rose from his chair and walked slowly toward the door. From within, a deep voice sounded. "Granted! Come forward, warrior!"

Cubal entered a huge room. It appeared to be a room similar to one once used by the ancient judges of the land called America. Cubal recalled seeing historical data on those days, including pictures that resembled this room. Seated behind the huge, elevated table were six men, all very old, including two who appeared frail, their beards white with age. The other four did not appear frail, but of them all, only two appeared to be capable of doing little more than living a sedentary lifestyle. His training though, kept him from assuming they were no danger to him. He knew better than to make such rash assumptions. The image of the old man who'd slapped him suddenly sprang to mind.

*These old men. Are they the warning?* He would not ignore those thoughts. His wariness of them increased.

The wood encasing the table had to be thousands of years in age. It was of ancient Earth days, an oak that was magnificently preserved. The chairs in which the men sat were also old. He could smell the musty odor of age within the room. Each of the men wore a black robe, though the clothing that peeked from beneath the robes of some of the men was different from the others.

Around the room, hung large pictures of individuals. Cubal recognized one of the pictures, that of an ancient Earth human called Washington. He recalled seeing the same picture in one of the in-depth historical training sessions every Wearer of the Black had to take. Each warrior was given condensed training on the history of the planets and inhabitants, and on some, the historical education was extensive. Earth's history had been one which had been very detailed. He realized that he was in a room that was probably used in the distant history of a place once called America.

He did a quick study of the six men, evaluating each one, calculating the potential threat they might pose, attempting to sense what hostilities lay in any of them toward him. His grey eyes swept slowly across the faces of each man. To his far left sat a man with a large black beard. His dark eyes peered intently at Cubal, and the warrior sensed in the man power and arrogance. The man's life force was strong.

Seated next to him was a man of slight stature, composed and serene in appearance, with long, flowing hair as white as the snows of Chor'ta, which stood in stark contrast to the inky darkness of his robes. The man's pale, almost milky eyes, stared with keen interest at Cubal. The warrior sensed no threat in the man, but did sense power.

*This is a man of secrets. Ancient secrets.* Cubal knew this man had the wisdom of ages within him. It glistened in his eyes, and radiated from his countenance.

The third man, seated next to the old, white-haired Ancient One, was slender, with a dark skin and darker eyes, and much younger than the others, though he too was clearly old. He sat motionless, his eyes riveted on their guest. Cubal sensed curiosity in the man, but no threat.

Next to him, near the center, sat a man who was studying him with an intensity that was unmatched by any of the others. The man's dark eyes were moving constantly, as though he distrusted his senses. He looked to the left and right of Cubal, then above him and back again, and rested finally upon Cubal's face. A slight smiled flickered briefly across the man's face and was gone. Cubal sensed great hostility from this one, although his swarthy features were now expressionless, hiding the mask of hatred that lurked within his being.

The man started to speak, but was interrupted by the man to Cubal's right, and seated on the end. He was a tall man, also white of hair, but with streaks of black on the sides, and no hair upon his face. His eyebrows were full and bushy, shadowing strange green eyes. "Cubal, allow me to introduce my friends." A smile creased the sallow face of the other, but the man's eyes were void of emotion.

"I am Joab. He pointed a bony finger to his right and said, "Here is Rey—sometimes we call him Mohammed—and beside him is Cra'et, then Mo'sathu, then Karl, and the ugly one at the end is called Testre."

He leaned back and continued, arms now folded across his chest. "Here, we have sought thee across the worlds, and suddenly, you come seeking us. What is it that called thee to us?"

"I was told of your quest for my presence. I come to know why you seek me. Now, tell me, for what purpose do you seek me?"

"From whence do you come, warrior?" Rey, the slender, dark-skinned man leaned forward, his brow wrinkled, his dark eyes staring intently at Cubal.

"I came from Na'ha."

"Did you stop elsewhere?"

"I stopped on Glale." *They know I was there.* He was not sure how they had tracked him, but they had known where he'd gone. It was as he had been told by Blythe.

"And what business had you there?" The old man continued his questioning.

"To assist a friend in trouble."

Rey looked at the man seated to his left, and a smile appeared on the face of the other.

Joab spoke in a deep bass voice in contrast to the sharp, high pitched tones of the slender Ancient One to his right. "Rey wonders what need there would have been to enlist a warrior such as yourself on Glale?"

Of all of them, Joab appeared to have a more youthful appearance, in spite of his obvious antiquity. His face was unwrinkled, and his hair, white with the streaks of black on the sides, belied the man's age. His hands were folded in front of him, and the man's green eyes were crinkled with friendliness and curiosity.

Cubal responded calmly, "One was there such as myself and another called Laird." *I must appear to them to be cooperative, and not afraid of their questions. Do they know of the special powers of Blythe and others on Glale?*

"I take it you were successful, then?" The man smiled.

Cubal allowed a wisp of a smile to trace itself across his lips. "I am here. They are gone from Glale."

The man grunted and whispered something to Mo'sathu. The other said, "I have no interest in what happens to Glale. My interest is in you. We have concluded that you are the perfect specimen for a special project we have."

Testre, the large, bearded man then spoke. His voice was guttural, low pitched, and almost a growl. "Mo'sathu babbles." He glared at the

109

other man, then peered intently at Cubal, and with an authoritative wave of his hand, said. "Step closer, man, that I can see you." His voice was that of a man used to being obeyed, used to command.

Cubal sensed the danger in the man. *He has slain many.* His wariness increased.

Cubal moved forward several feet and stopped. The man looked closely at Cubal for several long moments, then said, "I will not waste your time, warrior, babbling about other worlds and other wars. We have sought you because we want you to train our people in war. And, we also want you to command our Gating Force."

Cubal's response was quick and his words innocently mild. "War? I did not know of any wars on Earth. I had heard your former king had stopped all wars."

Suddenly, Karl, until now silent, and observing it all in a detached fashion, laughed, the noise a peculiar sound, very nasal. "He is no longer a king. He is gone, and good riddance. But, now the wolves have come to feed."

Cubal asked, "Against whom would I war?"

"Oh, yes, Karl, tell him, by all means." The bearded man named Testre was grinning as he leaned forwards, peering down the long wooden table at the other.

Karl ignored Testre, put two bony fingers to his lips, stopping just under his lower lip, and in careful, measured tones, said, "Enemies, warrior. Old enemies. They seek to destroy us, and we cannot permit that to happen." He tapped the fingers against his lower lip as he measured the man standing before him clad in the golden cloak. It was apparent the man was in deep thought, and carefully evaluating Cubal.

"And who are these enemies?" Again, Cubal's voice was soft and pleasant, his tone that of one mildly curious.

Cra'et, who'd sat quietly, observing Cubal intently, suddenly spoke, his voice resonating with command.

*This one has power.* Cubal was astonished that he'd not detected the man's force. He'd concealed himself well. *He knows some of the D'vru technique.*

"You shall work with us to destroy an enemy that is more deadly than any that has ever come upon the Earth. If they are not destroyed,

110

every one of them, they will end the human race. We will be raising an invasion force that shall destroy them, both here, and to the very throne of their leader. We shall bring the war to them and not wait for them to come to us. Already, there are those who await our command, and weapons are being prepared. You will be part of that invasion force."

The man shifted in his seat, and for a brief fraction of a second, his coat opened revealing the glimmer of a suit with a brilliant silver hue beneath the coat. *A Crelian stealth suit. This one has studied with the Crelians, the workers of black magic.*

They were a mysterious people, shadowy, seldom seen, and almost never discussed. Cubal had undergone some educational training on them in his early days, being told only that he was to avoid them if possible, and to beware if ever he engaged one of them in battle. They had mysterious powers, did works that, centuries ago, was called black magic, and were said to be assassins who never failed. Once they targeted a victim, that person died. They wore grey cloaks, though Cra'et apparently traded the grey for the black robes, and beneath the grey cloak, they always wore a silver suit which gave them strange powers—some said, invisibility. He wondered if it had some of the same properties of his cloak.

Cubal studied the man closely, absorbing everything emanating from the man's energies, testing, and feeling the power there. He did not fear the man, but he knew that with this one, he would have to be very careful. This man could hurt him.

Finally, he said, "I have no interest in your war."

The entire room was suddenly filled with a silence. Cubal sensed the tension in the room.

The man in the hidden silver suit said softly, his voice pregnant with menace: "You will, soon."

Cubal did not reply. They spoke amongst themselves for several minutes, then Karl asked, "Is it true that you were able to defeat C'chy'las, the Crs'ting?"

Cubal said quietly, "I know not such a person."

"But you fought in the Crs'ting Wars, did you not?"

"I did."

"And you fought directly with some of those creatures?"

"True." *Why does he ask me questions when he already knows the answer?*

"And was not one of them as yourself?"

"That is true."

"And was not that battle one which tested your skills as they'd never been tested?"

"True." *How could they know this? They seek something. What?*

The Ancient One named Karl allowed a slight smile to cross his leathery features, then looked at his companions and said to them, "He is here. C'chy'las is not." He chuckled softly. Then the group talked amongst themselves, this time in a language unknown to Cubal. He knew three thousand languages and six thousand dialects of those languages. But, this was not one which he'd ever heard. They continued talking, their whispers at times rising to levels of angry shouts.

Finally, the Ancient One called Mo'sathu turned and said, "We have prepared a place for you. Go and rest, and we shall talk again, later."

"A speech from you later will not change my mind." Cubal stood relaxed. He'd moved away from the large table to enable him to see better the entire room, especially the Ancient Ones. He did not like being so close to the one named Cra'et.

Suddenly, the room's far end was transformed into a bluish cloud. From the cloud stepped a man clad in a pale brown shirt that was loose upon the man. Matching pants billowed as the man walked. Cubal's eyes met the warm brown eyes of the stranger, and instantly, Cubal felt the danger in the man. But, more than that, he felt the presence of the most radiant force of raw power he'd ever known. This being appeared as a man, but Cubal knew he was something far more than that. The man strode toward Cubal. The warrior felt his defenses come into place, and instantly he was completely the warrior, fully alert, ready for battle.

"Be at rest, Cubal. I will do you no harm. I want peace, not battle with you." The voice was in stark contrast to the power Cubal sensed from this man. It was mellow and kindly. The man stopped several feet away, as though he knew that to come closer was to risk death.

"Who are you?" Cubal's question was delivered in a tone matching the stranger's tone of voice.

*This man wanted me to know his power.* Cubal was not disturbed by this thought, for on the Fifth Level of Control, there was nothing that could disturb the concentration of a warrior. He was the most focused being in the room at the moment. Nothing escaped his attention. He detected the seemingly idle gesture by the wearer of the silver suit, and knew it was preparatory to a move of some sort that would either bring attack from the man, or place him in a position to attack. Accordingly, Cubal's position altered ever so slightly.

"Rest, Cra'et!" The stranger's voice was not mellow, now. It was a command with a measure of power in the words. Cubal saw the one called Cra'et react instantly, settling back in his seat, the preparatory position gone. Instantly, the threats and hostilities that had moved him to a Level Five disappeared. He felt himself moving downward, and then he halted, keeping himself in a state of battle readiness at a Level Two, not trusting his senses completely.

The man turned to Cubal, and completely ignoring his question, said, "It is not merely that we want you to fight wars with us. Our desire is far more than that. We need warriors such as yourself, men who have been used by others and discarded, left to shift for themselves. We want men like you to rule over our worlds." He waved his hand suddenly, and the bluish cloud disappeared, then transformed itself into a giant screen of some sort, unlike anything Cubal had ever seen. There was detail and clarity in the view greater than even the screens of Choi, where one could see worlds and events of the past with the sense that one was there.

The stranger beckoned to Cubal. "Come. I wish to show you something."

The scene was a compelling one, and Cubal's curiosity was aroused. There was a sense of present-time reality to the scene before him. He moved closer, watching the small vessels flying through the air, and the activity of a city somewhere. It was not a familiar scene.

"This is the planet D'rath, home of the D'rathians. You know of them, do you not?"

Cubal nodded. He'd fought with them. They were responsible, it was said, for the origins of D'vru. They had been a separate unit in all of the Merged Forces, never integrating nor coming under the control of the War Council. They'd chosen their battles, and chose who they would fight with, and when. They had chosen Cubal and his contingent to fight with, and had been the group which had incurred the fewest losses in the war. Next to the Wearers of the Black, they'd inflicted the greatest casualties on the enemies. It was a warrior culture.

"Well, come. I must show you this." The man stepped into the scene, and instantly, Cubal saw the man standing on a small hill just overlooking the city. Cubal knew then that this was not merely a screen that gave the appearance of being in a place whilst walking amongst the scene, but was in fact some sort of transport device. Once you stepped into the scene, you were there, or so it seemed. Clearly, it was different from the visualization machines of the Choi'te.

He stepped into the scene, and found himself just behind the strange man whose back was to him. The man was gazing out at the city below. In a deep, resonant voice pitched almost to a whisper, he said, "This city is doomed for destruction unless you assist them. The Crs'tings, and a race of whom you do not know, shall attack this place in just a few years. The D'rathians shall lose the battle, for those who assist the Crs'tings are powerful, and far more deadly than even the Crs'tings. They are the Mir'jna. They have weapons that can destroy entire planets."

Cubal's interest was not apparent, and he betrayed nothing in his voice as he asked, "And how would they destroy a planet? Don't the D'rathians have shields in place?"

The man smiled. "Oh yes, they have shields. But, this device is something that is not affected by shields. It was developed by scientists working for the mining consortiums for crushing meteorites. The Crs'tings  discovered a way to use it to crush entire planets. This planet is on their schedule."

He paused for a long moment, then added, "Unless of course, you enlist in our cause to stop them."

Cubal replied, "I have sensed in you a power unlike any I have ever found in another human. I believe that you have the power in yourself to wage a war against the enemies of D'rath, or of Earth, for that matter. Your need for me is not apparent."

The man smiled, then said, "I will not bother to explain for now, but I cannot leave Earth, except in a device such as this, which projects a portion of our being to the point at which the device is tuned. We are on D'rath, but only in our consciousness. We have a form field which encapsulates our consciousness, and it permits us to walk about and see, but we are invisible to those on the planet, and we are limited in what we can do in this form.

"We can, for instance, influence those on the planet, by speaking to them. They will not realize that we are speaking to them, but they often will act according to what we say to them. They believe, of course, that it is their own thoughts, but in fact, it is our voice which directs them." The man turned away from the scene and toward Cubal, a congenial smile on his face.

"You created this device?" Cubal was staring intently at the other.

"In part, yes. But, I did have help. The idea was mine. I understood the laws that govern such things and knew it was possible. It took me a long time to perfect it, though." The man was clearly proud of his accomplishment.

"This is a device that could have saved many lives during the Time of Wars."

"Oh, but it did." He paused for a long moment as though hesitant about revealing the next bit of information, then added, "Have you never wondered why the Crs'tings abandoned Earth and fled?"

Cubal raised his eyebrows. "You did that?"

The man smiled, and Cubal felt himself drawn to this man, felt himself liking him. There was something appealing about the man. His almost boyish good looks were offset by his penetrating brown eyes, which gave the promise of a friendship and bond that was unbreakable.

"Yes. I learned their speech and imaged them. Then, I practiced with several Crs'tings we captured here on Earth. After that, we sought them out and spoke words to them that filled them with terror."

Cubal allowed the smallest of smiles to cross his face. "I have wondered why they fled. I knew it was not me, nor those who joined with me in the battle. They could have won, had they stayed and fought. We were losing too many battles. Excepting for the D'rathians, and my special unit, everyone else was taking huge casualties."

The man smiled. "We know. We also know that they sent their best warrior at you. He was on Earth, and was to have been the one set up on Earth to rule. You destroyed him, and that was the beginning of the end for them, for I used the news of his destruction and certain other messages to terrorize them. They became convinced that there was an army just like you. We knew, of course, that there was but one like you."

Cubal raised his eyebrows as he studied the speaker. *It makes more sense than the god story Blythe believes.*

Cubal asked suddenly, "Who are you?"

The sudden shift did not surprise the other. He remained as cordial as ever and replied, "I am Lucien, Warrior of Light." The man made an ancient, polite little bow of his head toward Cubal, then straightened, and extended his hand in the Earth handshake. Cubal paused, staring deeply into the other's eyes, probing. Then he held his hand out and took the hand of the other. They shook, and it was a strange, surrealistic feeling since he knew the body he was in was not really his, and the hand he was shaking was not real.

He followed the man, and suddenly they were back in the room they'd left. Everyone was seated as they were when he'd left.

Lucien's power was now shielded from him, and Cubal no longer felt the threats. The man stepped up closer to him and said, "Will you help us, warrior?" He stared deep into the eyes of Cubal and the warrior felt himself drawn to the man. He added, "The Crs'tings come, warrior."

Cubal looked around the room at the others. Only from Cra'et did he feel hostility, and something in him knew that there could never be trust or friendship between himself and that one. But, he'd been with many armies and in many circumstances where he'd worked and fought alongside beings for which he had little use or respect. They were comrades in arms. Their unity was in their cause. They did not have to like one another.

He looked back at Lucien and said, "I will hear what you have to say." He paused, looked back at Cra'et and then back to Lucien and added, "But know this: I am my own man. I serve no master nor gods. If I serve in a cause, in your cause, I will serve in a manner that suits me, not you."

Lucien smiled. "I would have it no other way."

Cra'et stood suddenly and said loudly, "No! I will not have this dog coming and declaring to us his rights. He will serve, and he will obey as any other soldier; and he will be subject to the Council's orders!"

Cubal felt the man's threat, and saw the beginnings of his movements of death. Cubal instantly went to the Fifth Level, and moved away from Lucien. He said softly, "Do not interfere, and stay away from me for anything close to me shall die." With that, he moved into the middle of the room.

Cra'et leaped over the high barrier between them and landed like a big cat. There was no sound of his landing. He began the slip-slide of the Terthian fighters, combined with the hand movements of the Clythian assassins. But, that was not what alerted Cubal. Those were ancient forms of combat, and though deadly to most, were mere inconveniences to one trained in the ways of D'vru. It was the absence of sound. A warrior in the Fifth Level of control will hear every whisper of sound. And, there had been no sound from the ghost that stalked him.

Suddenly, Cubal shot straight up into the air, rolling in the spin maneuver that had stunned Antal. He spun to the far side of the room. As he moved, he saw the image of the one that had been advancing toward him disappear, and another image appeared directly behind where he'd been.

*That is why I heard no sound. The suit produces illusions and dampens sound.*

But the image directly behind where he'd been was no illusion, and was slicing the air with a short beam Ra'd gun.

Cubal now knew the secret of the Crelian suit. It enabled them to project illusions and somehow altered the senses to give them invisibility. Cubal moved closer to the wall, aware now that Cra'et would be closing on him, cloaked by his suit. There were four attack points with his back to the wall instead of the multiples of attack points away from the wall. He waited for a long second, watching as Cra'et whirled around and moved toward him, then disappeared, only to appear suddenly to his left, against the wall and moving quickly toward him. He knew his enemy was attempting to draw him out, and that the approaching visions were mere images.

Cubal leaped toward the center of the room with the speed only achieved by those who'd mastered every level of D'vru. His move was the beginning of a maneuver that was for those battles where one was surrounded by enemies and where visual contact was minimal. It required constant, explosive movement. In less than a second, he was near the center of the room, then back near where he'd left, then a leap into the air, then back to the wall and out again. As he moved, his hands were a blur of motion, whipping through the air at invisible targets.

Suddenly, there was a flash of silver and Cra'et stumbled against a wall, gasping. Blood rushed from the side of his head. He slid down the wall, his breath coming heavily. Cubal continued to move. He knew he'd hit the Crelian, but he was not certain that what he saw lying against the wall was Cra'et. He'd learned long ago to rely on all his senses, so, although his eyes were telling him Cra'et was there and possibly seriously wounded, he was not certain. He moved away again, back to the center, then moved near where the Crelian lay, and with a speed that would not permit a counterattack, flicked a stiffened hand against the shoulder. It was firm, and the man fell to one side.

Instantly, Cubal stopped his moves and walked quickly to the side of the Crelian. Cra'et's eyes were open, staring at Cubal, and his breathing was labored. He whispered, "What manner of warrior is it that can move as you move? How could you know?"

He struggled for a moment, coughed, then continued, "Nothing in the studies revealed that you had knowledge of our ways. You should not have known of my illusion."

"Even had you been able to trick me, I would have stopped you, for as you pulled the weapon from your cloak, its sounds were as thunder in my ears. Didn't your studies about me reveal that to you?"

The other attempted to laugh, but only coughed. "Yes, but I did not believe it. We are not known for our clumsiness, and silence is our power. We are the death never seen and never heard"

Lucien stepped forward and knelt beside the fallen Crelian. "Until now. Your unbelief and your foolishness has cost you dearly, Cra'et.

You shall be sent to your home to recover. Your wounds are not fatal, though that was chance only, for had you not been falling away when the blow came, you would surely be dead." Lucien's voice lowered and he said softly, "You played the fool."

He beckoned for a man standing near the door to tend to Cra'et, then turned to Cubal and said, "I apologize for Cra'et's actions. I do not know what possessed him to act in such a fashion."

Cubal shrugged. "It is unimportant."

Lucien stepped back and began walking away, a slight smile forming on his lips. He stopped, looked back and said, "Would you come with me so we can talk in private? We have many things to discuss, and it is important that we have no more interruptions from fools." The smile had gone from his lips.

Cubal followed silently.

He knew what Lucien wanted.

And, he knew his answer.

Cubal, Wearer of the Gold, would fight in the cause of Lucien, Warrior of Light.

It appeared to be a war worthy of his efforts.

He doubted though, that Blythe would call it a god event.

# Chapter 11

*"Dialog with an enemy is like wrestling a cloud. Substance is there but it is impossible to grasp that substance."* D'VRU, *BOOK ONE: The Senses*

Cubal could not recall a time when he'd been more thoroughly entertained. Lucien was a treasure of knowledge and wit. He found him to be more than pleasant company. There was a feeling of companionship after the first hour of conversation with the man. But, he was still wary. He'd sensed the raw power of the man earlier, and though Lucien had radiated nothing but good will since that time, Cubal remembered. And, he still was unsure of exactly what Lucien wanted with him.

They were seated in a small room, two walls lined with ancient books. The room had a musky smell to it, no doubt emanating from the old books. On another wall was a large blank screen. He wondered if it were similar to the one he'd walked through earlier. At the north end was a small area with soft, cushioned seating using the newer anti-grav devices that made one feel much lighter in the chair. An ancient fireplace was nearby, something Cubal had seen in training, but had never witnessed in operation. It was a simple device, taking wood pieces as its fuel, channeling the smoke through a vent at the top called a chimney. The heat radiated outwards from the fireplace. Cubal wondered if Lucien really had a need for such a device. For himself, it was a pleasant thing, but he did not need the heat from the flames to maintain his body heat. He could regulate that himself.

"From what source did your golden cloak come? It looks marvelous." Lucien reached over and stroked the fabric softly once, smiled, and leaned back into his chair. "Nice. Very nice."

"A friend gave it to me."

"Oh? An expensive gift. I have never seen its like." Lucien settled deeper into the chair, clasped his hands together, leaned slightly forward, studied Cubal closely for a long moment, then asked, "So have you considered my offer?"

Cubal leaned forward slightly and replied, "Yes, but I cannot respond, because I do not know enough yet."

"What more must you know?"

"Who you are."

Lucien was silent, his black eyes probing deep into Cubal's eyes, his face an emotionless mask hiding the thoughts of the man. Finally, he said, "You believe me to be some sort of evil god or devil, don't you?"

"Devils and gods I know not. That you are a powerful being, I know. I simply do not know yet what manner of being you are."

Lucien smiled. "Good, for I am neither devil nor god. As for having power, this is true. I have learned about power and have acquired it. I have learned many things in the long years I have lived, and.... "

Cubal interrupted, "How many years is that? Years, you've lived?"

Lucien's eyebrows raised as he pondered the answer to the question. He said slowly, "I would only say several thousand of Earth's years. I do not keep track of such things."

"Are you what is called an immortal?"

Lucien laughed, his glistening white teeth contrasting with the deeply tanned skin tones. "Immortal is a word that seeks to embody a concept first imagined by religious fanatics striving to enthrone a man they wished to call god. They believed, and still do, that this god could give them immortality—life forever." He paused, then, with a small grin, added, "Of course, all they had to do was swear allegiance, and worship this god in order to get it."

"So, would this be such a large price to pay for such a great gift?"

Lucien shook his head. "No, of course not. And that is the point. This delusion is passed from generation to generation, but it is a false hope." Lucien rubbed his hands together and held them out toward the fireplace. "But, perhaps it is not such a bad false hope. After all, if it keeps one happy and content, then I am for that."

Cubal found himself liking the man in spite of his reservations. He was saying things that made a lot of sense. Their position on gods was closer than anyone he'd ever talked to before. He asked, "Lucien, why did you say I thought you to be a god or devil?"

The man came from his faraway look slowly. "But, didn't you think so?"

"No. I told you, I have no such beliefs."

"Well, I suppose it had to do with the fact that we know you stopped on the planet Glale. There are some there who hold strongly to this belief system. I assumed you had spoken with them, and that they may have tried to convince you that because I was not of them and their persuasion, I might be a devil of some sort." He laughed softly, shaking his head at the thought.

Cubal smiled. "Yes, they did tell me of one who lives on this planet, and who is evil, and opposes them and their god. I respect them and their ways, but I cannot accept their ideas about their god. And thus, I must reject their concept of a devil, though they did not mention you by name. Are you the same as the one called Lucifer?"

Lucien sat up straight and his tanned face broke into a broad grin. "Me? Lucifer?" The man's laughter was hearty, and lasted for a full minute. He swept his fingers through his lush, black hair and said, "Lucifer is a mythical creature of the religious imagination used to scare their children into following them into their beliefs. I am no doubt perceived by some to be this Lucifer, or the mythical creature called Satan, but that is merely a fiction created by those who would snare and enslave generations of humans."

Lucien's face lost its grin as he pursed his lips and added, "Frankly, I can see that it has been a useful myth for them."

He frowned and leaned slightly forward, then asked, "Did they tell you that you would meet up with such a mythical creature here on Earth?"

"It was implied that we would meet."

Lucien shook his head slowly. "I am sorry to disappoint you my friend. I am not the devil you seek, indeed, if that is who you seek. I am but a man who has managed to prolong his life by use of a special DNA substance that renews the body tissues. It is an ancient formula. Those you saw in the room have knowledge of this formula, and have used it to prolong their own lives, though some of them have need to renew themselves soon, and one is coming to his end, even with the formula. He has been with me for a long, long time."

Cubal nodded his head in understanding. "I too, have benefited from this science. I have not the life-span of yourself, and have lived around two hundred of your Earth years. However, I do not perceive any diminishment of my strength as the years pass, and was told during my time of training that I would live for many hundreds of Earth years."

The other smiled. "You are but a child." Lucien took a deep breath, stared at Cubal for a long moment, then continued: "Let me tell you how it came to be that I became, in the minds of some religious types, this mythical creature they call Lucifer." He settled back into his chair, put his fingers together in a steeple and stared into the fireplace. His voice was low as he spoke.

"Thousands of years ago there arose a group of people on Earth who I came to know quite well. I'm not sure of their origins, but many believe they had their beginnings with a co-mingling of human seed with that of an alien race whose nature was antagonistic to mankind. They were called Israelites, or Jews, and by some, Hebrews. These people were a warrior race, very disciplined, and ruthless in their dealings with those they perceived to be enemies."

He chuckled as memories came to him, then added in a rueful tone, "Which seemed to be just about everyone around, including me, now and then, although I did ride with them from time to time. We fought together and enjoyed one another's company, but things would change, leaders would change, and those I once rode with, rode against me. Eventually, I found myself and my people bitter enemies of many of these Jews, though that would change, in time."

Lucien gazed for a long moment at the fireplace, his lips pursed, as he remembered old time. He continued. "In those early days, it really depended on who came into power. When certain ones came into power who were evil, they tended to see everyone else, even some of their own, as enemies. These are the ones, these evil kings, and those who declared themselves to be what they called prophets, or seers, that is, men who allegedly could see this mystical god, and who purportedly spoke with him at times—these are the ones who came up with the concepts of devils, and this mystical, all-powerful god."

Lucien paused, lifted his face to the ceiling and with an expression of mock fear, added, "A god whom I have never seen, by the way." The last words were hissed, and the contempt he felt was evident.

Then, his mercurial personality wiped away that persona, and with a slight smile and a wave of his hands, implying that was all insignificant to him, Lucien leaned forward and continued. "I acquired some very ancient secrets back then, including the secret to long life. As a result, I became a very powerful enemy to them, for I knew these people better than anyone knew them. As they became strong, they sought to subjugate every nation around them, including me and those people with whom I lived.

"As I mentioned earlier, when certain of their leaders came into power, we became bitter enemies. But, there arose other leaders who were visionaries, men who saw through the nonsense and babble of these self-anointed prophets of their invisible god. These men I could work with, and we had peace between us in their days. Indeed, with some of those leaders, we actually rode together and fought common enemies together. But, even in those days, there was always a core group within those people who hated me and sought to undermine my relationship with others within the nation."

Lucien looked away from Cubal and stared at the floor for a long moment, then looked up and with a smile on his face, added, "It was during this time that the myth of this creature called Satan was born. Someone, I'm not sure who, came up with the idea of inventing this dark and mysterious creature with fantastic powers, who is responsible for all the bad things that happen to them."

A slight grin lift the corners of his mouth, as he continued, "Frankly, I have to admit that it was brilliant propaganda. So now, these Jews could do all the evil they wanted to do and blame it on this imaginary Satan creation. Someone also took my name, Lucien, and linked it to this mythical Satan, so for many centuries, I have been a devil in the eyes of many."

He lost the little smile that had come to his face, and with a serious look in his eyes, asked, "Have you ever read their magic book?"

Cubal raised his eyebrows. "You mean the book they call Bible?" Without waiting for an answer, he shook his head. "No. I have read pieces of it, and we were given outlines dealing with the myth, along with some of the history and the beliefs, but I was never interested in delving deeply into the book. There was no need. We were taught about many religions, their tenets, their basic structure and so forth. This was but one of thousands. Some of the words of their book were included in our instructions, but all of it was merely to acquaint us with religions in order to...."

"In order to evaluate the strengths and weaknesses of those who hold to a particular belief system, so as to better evaluate them as an opponent." Lucien's face was a broad smile now and it was clear he delighted in finishing the thought.

Cubal smiled. "Or friend. We wished to know our friends as well. But, we did not need to know the whole of the religion—just enough to do the evaluation of strengths and weaknesses."

Lucien's smile left his face and he said quickly, "Well, you have missed nothing in your education by not reading the thing. If you ever read it, you would see that this book of theirs ascribes to me powers that I can only wish I had. It puts me as a one-time partner with this mythical god of theirs, and then gives me credit for every heinous crime ever perpetuated upon humans and the universe itself."

Lucien signed deeply, leaned back with his hands locked behind his head, then added, "But, it is true, I did lay waste to their cities and people from time to time." He smiled as though recalling with fondness, those days. "However, the attacks were made upon me and my cities first."

Lucien removed his hands from behind his head, rubbed them together and said, "But, never have I been unjust with them. Never once. Year after year, they maligned me, and ascribed to me their own evil deeds. It became laughable, actually. They were like that. They always had someone else to blame for their misery. They even blamed their own god. Really!" He shook his head slowly, and his lips pursed as old memories came back to him.

Suddenly, Lucien got very animated and his eyes were widened as they expressed incredulity. He extended his hands, palm upwards, arched his eyebrows, then continued, "When others nations attacked them, these Jews often ascribed these attacks as coming from their god as punishment because they did not pay homage to him as he insisted." Lucien's eyes crinkled and the grin on his face was followed by soft laughter, accompanied by a slow shaking of his head in disbelief.

Cubal asked, "But what of this Messiah? It is said that he was slain for the evils of this people and that he returned to life after being dead for three days. I have seen the historical viewer of his alleged return to life. Is he the same god of the Jews, or is he a different one?"

Lucien's face grew serious. He leaned forward, put his elbows upon his knees, folded his hands, and began speaking, his voice matter-of-fact. "Well, it is true that that someone—a man called Jesus—was placed upon a piece of wood, which at the time was a rather crude method of execution."

He grinned, then added, "They tried to ascribe that deed to me as well, but if I'd had a hand in such a thing, I'd have merely put a sword through the man and been done with the matter. I do not enjoy watching a man be tortured."

A flicker of something, Cubal was not quite sure, came across the man's face and into his eyes. Lucien appeared to discount the things that had taken place between himself and this race called Jews, but Cubal was not so sure now. Something still troubled the man about those days, something that bothered Lucien deeply.

*He controls an anger that lurks beneath. No, it is a rage he controls. Yes. A rage.* Cubal studied Lucien carefully as he wondered at the tumultuous history between this man and the Jews.

Lucien shook his head slowly, and his mouth turned down in an exaggerated display of disgust. "They really were quite ignorant, and barbaric in those days, you know. This Jesus claimed to have a virgin birth...." Lucien burst out laughing suddenly, and it was several moments before he stopped.

He regained his composure and continued, "A virgin birth? Ha! I happened to know the woman who birthed this Jesus. She was a Temple Prostitute." He paused for a long moment, as though he were hesitant to add another thought, then added, "Even I've been with her."

He swept his fingers through his dark hair and said, "But, virgins and such nonsense aside, consider that this man who would be god came to Jerusalem and attempted to take over the place, and made a claim to be a god!"

Lucien's voice rose as he ended the sentence, and as he continued, he said with a tinge of exasperation, one hand stretched toward Cubal: "They merely gave the fool what he obviously wanted: the death penalty. Fortunately for him, one of his followers was able to slip him a potion that enabled him to sleep as one dead. Then later, they came and extracted him from the tomb he was laid in and nursed him back to health. Of course, his followers declared him to be risen from the dead and living on a mythical planet called Heaven."

The dark-haired man wiped a hand across his lips, as though wiping at an invisible irritant. He continued: "The followers of this Jesus were called Christians. They've long since disappeared, and the movement died out as soon as he disappeared from Earth."

Lucien folded his hands across his chest as he leaned back in his chair, took a deep breath and continued. "Before this Jesus began ruling the planet, the Jews hated him, but embraced him after he took over. They knew opposition to him was fatal, so what choice had they? Previously, they hated him. They wanted to keep the mysterious god they'd created in the beginning, and didn't like the competition.

"Frankly, they were both pathetic gods, in my opinion, since they never did anything for anyone, that I could see. Indeed, who has even seen the god of the Jews? And the god of Christians, well, he was no god, but a man who knew some secrets, just as I do."

Lucien was grinning now as he continued, "After a long period of time of waiting and using the potion of life I told you about, the same potion I take, this man who supposedly died and rose back from death, was able to take over this planet and rule the world. And rule he did—with an iron fist. Indeed, he and his forces of evil combined their powers against me and forced me into hiding for many long years. I hid deep within the bowels of Earth until we were strong enough to drive them from power. That was no easy chore, believe me, for he had entrenched himself upon the world, and the slavish devotion of his followers made it difficult, but we did prevail. He left with the use of a transport device."

With a look of disgust, he added, "And now we are attempting to undo the harm he brought with his futile attempt to create worshipers of himself." A dark intensity came over the man.

Cubal folded his arms across his chest as he relaxed more in the chair. "So, it was indeed this same Christ who appeared to die, who then returned and ruled here for a millenium. But, did he not do good things in his rule?"

"Oh, of course. He was a genius, especially at getting people to follow him. But, they were all slaves. There is no other way to put it. He had devices that affected the minds of the people and made them docile. They were mere robots. The people, indeed, even me, were imprisoned against our wills. Actually, it was his evil that created the device that keeps me bound to this planet."

"Where is this device, and how does it work?"

Lucien shook his head. "I do not know. I only know that I cannot go beyond the atmosphere of Earth. The device yet operates." He smiled suddenly and said, "Perhaps you can find it and destroy it. Would that be something that you would do for me?"

Cubal was silent for a long moment, then replied, "Perhaps. I do not think it right that he trap you like that. Did you give him cause for such?"

"Cause? Well, if you call refusing to call him god, refusing to bend my knee, and refusing to accept his ways, then yes, I gave him cause, and will continue to give him cause. Indeed, I know where he went when he fled this planet, and with your help, and the assistance of other very special beings I have at my command, I will one day invade his home and bring him down. He will feel my wrath. This I promise."

Cubal sensed the anger, the rage in the man, and knew it threatened to take over the man's control. His face discolored and darkened, and his eyes narrowed as they stared into the fire.

Suddenly, he lost the faraway look and regain control of the rage. Lucien turned his head to Cubal, and in a calm, matter-of-fact voice, asked, "Have you renewed yourself, yet?"

"I do not understand what you mean."

"If you do not renew your cells every three hundred years, you will begin to age as any mortal. Some may be able to hold out longer, but the usual time is three hundred years."

"I have never heard of such a thing. I was only told that I would not age as others, but that I could die as others, and if I did not perish in battle, one day I would die of old age."

Lucien smiled. "When you join us, I will take you to our Center for Life. They will give you an injection, or a pill, if you prefer. It is not a difficult process, except that once you take it, you must rest yourself for a full ten hours with absolutely no exertion. It is in this time that the process begins to work on the cells, but if you are moving about and exerting energies, it will not be as effective, and may not work at all."

Cubal thought for a long moment, then said, "I would like that. However, I will need to study the formula completely. I am careful about the things I ingest."

"Are you not able, once you ingest something, to control the disbursement of the elements of that food or drink?"

Cubal said, "You have studied my history well."

"Very much. Thus, if there is anything ingested by a wearer of the black, he is able to expel it in several ways, or even to neutralize it with acids from the stomach."

"This is true." He smiled at the other and said, "I suppose that I will accept your pill, but I still wish to look at it closely."

"Good. Now tell me some things I don't know."

Cubal asked, "Such as?"

"I know your strengths to some measure. I do not know your full capabilities. I must know them if I am to resource you appropriately. I need to know, for example, what assistance to give you in battle, how many forces, what kinds of weapons, that sort of thing." He paused, then added, "And, I must know your weaknesses."

*He moves swiftly. Why?* The questions troubled Cubal, though he was not sure why. These were things that any commander would want to know. Indeed, in the wars, he had been asked similar questions by more than one commander. He had always responded.

*I cannot reveal this information.* The thought came in a flicker before his response. "My strengths you know. They have not changed, nor have I changed. We do not change. As for my weaknesses, I am vulnerable to a great many things."

"Have you mastered Ex'tal's dimensional shift yet?"

*He knows. How?* He replied, "I have observed that. I asked to speak to one man there, but was told it was forbidden."

"I can teach it to you. It is an easy thing to master. It takes concentration, an easy thing for someone who has been taught to control his mind as you have been taught." Lucien leaned back in his chair and continued, "Do you have any new strengths that you have developed?"

*Is this one also a reader of minds?* He kept his mental shield up. "I have refined my skills, and am better at some things now than before. I have learned many things from many people. So, my strengths are better now. Just use the data you have on me, then factor in experience and time. That will closely approximate what I can do. I know my evaluations are on file somewhere, for your questions are similar to ones asked me several times in years past. Always, my answers were the same, and today, those answers remain."

Lucien's face broke into a large smile, he slapped his knee and said, "Well good! I am pleased to know that you are a better warrior than before. I could see improvements in the Great Hall today. Your moves were quicker, more certain."

"You are very good to be able to detect such a thing. I did not know I had ever been observed by you in battle." *Where has he seen me before?* The thought bothered him.

Lucien smiled. "I have had years of experience, and have watched tens of thousands of hours of history. You are in some of that history."

Cubal hesitated a bit, as if afraid to ask his question, then softly, he asked, "Lucien, what would you do if I stood and left you, and refused to enter your war?"

The man was silent for a long time, studying the face of Cubal. Finally, he said, "Nothing, I suppose. I believe I could stop you, of course, even though you have great power and skills unequal to any man I've ever seen. But, I want you with me, not fighting me. So, I suppose I would hope that you would change your mind later and enlist in my cause, for it is a just cause."

Cubal stared at the man. It was the perfect answer. If he'd detected the slightest irritation, or anger, or resistance, he'd determined he would do exactly that: leave.

Cubal smiled. "You interest me, Lucien. You interest me in ways I do not yet understand, for I have never met someone quite like you before. I sense there is much more to you than I can see or hear. So, I shall remain here to learn more about you."

Lucien returned the smile, rose quickly to his feet and leaned forward, his hand extended. The two shook hands, and Lucien patted Cubal on the shoulder. "Cubal, it is rare that I call those who work for me, 'friend.' With a few rare exceptions, they are subordinate and never do I call them friend. I am very particular about who I bestow that upon." His hand squeezed Cubal's hand and he said softly, "Welcome aboard, my friend."

Cubal sensed the emotions in the man, and a strong feeling of friendship swept over him. He felt himself strangely drawn to this man. *Here was a man to fight with. To fight for.* The thought echoed in his mind as they left the room.

Cubal, Wearer of the Gold, was about to be a Warrior for Lucien, Warrior of Light.

# Chapter 12

*"What comes before the eyes seeks a place within the mind,
but what comes before the eyes should not always enter the
mind."* D'VRU, BOOK ONE: The Senses

For three days, Cubal did little more than talk with Lucien and
take a personally guided tour of vast complexes, some buried deep
beneath the Earth, others on isolated worlds, unnamed, unknown
and unseen by others. All of these visits were made without leaving
the main quarters. As before, he walked through a transporter of
some strange sort and explored, unseen and unhindered by walls
or barriers. The more he saw, the more impressed he was by the
enormity of Lucien's empire and the power the man wielded. It
became obvious that although there were various governments on
Earth, the real power lay with this man. The only place upon Earth
that seemed completely resistant to his powers was Jerusalem, the
former headquarters of the apparently now-departed Messiah.

The subject came up on the third day. Cubal had noticed that this
was a city never mentioned by Lucien, and he'd never seen it scanned,
viewed, or visited, yet every other major city was visible on the giant
screens that dotted one huge room they visited.

"Why no monitoring or visiting of Jerusalem?" asked Cubal.

There was no immediate response. The two were walking down
a long corridor. Lucien stopped finally and said, "They have sensing
devices there which would alert them to my actions. I will one day
absorb that city. But, the time is not yet come."

"In all these years, you have been unable to penetrate its barriers?"

Lucien's face flushed, and he answered in a terse voice, "I did not say I could not penetrate its barriers. I said the time was not right. They would become alerted to me, to my presence."

"And if they are alerted, what then? Does it matter? I must know their power to resist you if I am to fight against them." Cubal stared intently at Lucien.

"They have power and they can resist. But, their power is limited. We have engaged in many wars, and they do not always remain in the city."

"Are these beings called resurrected ones?"

Lucien smiled. "You have heard of such beings, then?"

"Yes. I do not believe such a thing is possible, but I have heard of them."

"Well, there are many there who are as ancient as myself, and they have power. Their problem is that they do not know how to use their power. Instead, they seek to abuse it by forcing their beliefs upon all of us, and seeking to enslave us for their god. I will resist their efforts to the death."

"Can they die?"

"What an interesting question. What prompted it?"

"Well, if they are resurrected beings, having died, what would it take to kill such a being? I must know if I am ever to battle with such beings."

Lucien's smile was wide with delight. "Many who follow them can die. And, there are some with them who are immortal only in that they refuse to expose themselves to real warfare. When you do battle with them, it is an image, an incredibly real image. And, just when you think they are defeated, that you have killed one, they arise as though from the dead. But, it is all illusion. Do not be deceived."

The dark one was silent for a brief moment, as his thoughts formed, then finally he added, "This is why we must one day go to their lair. We must reach into their homes, into their world. It is there that we will find this false god Messiah, and those who project themselves into our world."

Cubal did not respond. He was remembering his attack upon Blythe. That had been no image. He knew what had been before him, and remembered what he had felt and sensed. It was very real, and the flesh that he'd stuck was very solid, and no illusion. He could not refuse the reality of that event. He did not understand it, but one thing he knew: there was no projection, nor image of a man before him on that day. He'd struck down a living, breathing human. And, that human had risen as though nothing had happened.

On the fourth day, Cubal saw something that disturbed him. He was taken to a room of archives. Lucien spoke aloud in the room, obviously to a digital servant: "Show us the Time of the Troubles. Instantly, a huge, real-dimension display sprang into the center of the room, and Cubal found himself viewing a miniaturized display of a city. He could see people moving about and ancient flying machines called airplanes in the sky. This was a historical visage of some great, olden city.

"Now watch, warrior, and you will see those peace lovers, those who claim to be so docile. Watch what occurs."

Suddenly, from the air came a giant whooshing noise, and he watched as an entire city disappeared—vaporized. The scene suddenly shifted to another large city, and within a few seconds, the scene was duplicated. Then, a scene came up that showed a large contingent of soldiers. They were an impressive array of men and weapons. And then suddenly, they were all dead.

The device was shut down, and Lucien said, "This was all done by those who called themselves followers of Messiah—Christians." The last word was hissed and a slight curl appeared on Lucien's upper lip.

"When did this occur?"

"This was before your time. This was when the one who seeks to be a god used his powers to destroy much of humanity, and rule the Earth. We were attacked without warning and without mercy. It was the time I was forced to hide beneath the earth."

"If he had such powers, why did he not use them to maintain his position?"

Lucien smiled. "Because we developed more powers than he had. We were able to force him to leave Earth and hide out there amongst the stars." His hand swept upward and he pointed up.

134

Cubal was silent. He had seen many history projections. He'd never seen these before. They were of a clarity and detail that suggested that someone had been very close to the scene in order to have captured such quality images. Idly, he wondered how they survived such a cataclysmic event.

He'd informed Lucien that he would volunteer in the war. The tipping point for Cubal had been the fact that the Crs'tings were on the list of enemies, and that they were getting ready for another invasion. Cubal knew that so long as he lived, he would be enemy to these aliens. They were merciless and evil, and he would enlist in any war against them.

On the fifth day, Cubal was summoned to the large hall in which he'd first met the Ancient Ones. He entered the room as before, formally announced, the huge doors swinging wide, and an escort to the center of the room. This time, there was a different feel to the room. There was no hostility, no tension, and the faces of those looking down from their lofty seats were smiling at him. The seat of the silver-suited Ancient One was empty.

Karl said, "Welcome, Cubal, Wearer of the Black, and now of the Gold. We, of the Lord of Light, welcome you into our ranks. You are summoned this day to take the oath and to receive your commission. Stand forth!" The words rang out loudly in the large room and reverberated throughout the room.

A small man came up and knelt before him, his hands outstretched. In the hands was a medallion, silver and ebony in color, shaped much like the rays of a star, pointed on the ends. In the center was a single eye of ruby. Cubal removed the medallion off the red pillow and held it in his hand. A slender chain of golden hue was also with the medallion.

"You will wear the medallion when you are here, or when you must travel. It will grant you many privileges as you travel. It will unlock doors. No place will be barred to you, so long as you're wearing this. In battle, you will place the medallion in a safe pouch. You must never enter battle wearing the medallion, but you must take it with you wherever you go." The voice trailed off, and Cubal could hear the soft echo of whispers between several of the members of the Council.

Finally, a second voice sounded: "Cubal, do you swear your allegiance against all enemies of Lucien and the Council, and that you shall wage unrelenting war against all enemies of Lucien and the Council?" If this is so, then affirm.

Cubal replied, "I will wage war against all enemies, unrelenting, sparing not. This I affirm."

*So long as your enemies are mine.* The thought came unbidden.

Again, there was a flurry of whispers, then finally, a third voice sounded: "Then, a warrior for Lucien, Warrior of the Light, you are now, and forever more!"

The room darkened, and suddenly, the Council was gone and Cubal was alone in the room. He turned and left. In his room, he pondered the events. Lucien seemed sincere. Cubal was trained to detect a wide range of emotions, and deception was something one with his training could detect instantly. None of that was in Lucien. But, Cubal was uncomfortable with being an adversary to Blythe and Nathan.

He concluded that Lucien was as Barcel and simply did not understand their true nature. He knew the real enemy was the Crs'tings, and since they were enemy to Lucien, he would war in Lucien's cause. Indeed, Lucien seemed to be more ready to take the war to the Crs'tings than Blythe and his mythical god. But, he still could not dismiss the feeling of uneasiness he had.

Several days later, Lucien came to his room. The man stepped quietly through the door, handed him a small book and said, "Read this carefully. You will be taken from here in a vessel and dropped off on the side of a small hillside. This booklet will detail facts that you need to know about the city you will see ahead. It is a city where Crs'tings have landed. They have adopted the ways of the followers of this one who calls himself Messiah and they mingle freely with the disciples of this would-be god. Indeed, they are allied with the Crs'ting. You will be told what to do once you are in the city. Do not deviate in the slightest. And, do not be deceived by their easy, friendly manner. They are capable of great evil. Remember, it is this same group which enslaved an entire planet for one thousand years, bending them to the iron will of their master."

Cubal took the small booklet from his hand and nodded. He did not speak. Lucien left without further comment. The warrior moved to one of the several anti-grav chairs in the room and sat down to read. The language of the book was written in an old, obscure language called English, a language he'd learned as a child, but seldom used. In exquisite detail, the book outlined the city, showing its trails, roads, waterways, even who lived in what dwelling, with those who were deemed enemies shown in a glowing red, and those in the city who were friendly to Lucien, in a glowing green. The booklet explained the inner workings of the city, and then it gave his mission. He was to accompany a small force and take control of the city.

He finished the book, confident that he would recall every detail about the city, every street, and even the elevations, when he needed that information. He wondered why the city was deemed to be so important. It did not appear to be a large city. He assumed it had some strategic value. It did not seem to Cubal to be a difficult task to take the city. That could be done in a few hours, and if he could plan the attack, neither side would lose a single life. He could infiltrate the city, gain control of its key defenses, shut them down, then render each defensive contingent within the city helpless with a bit of special gas. He could incapacitate the city within four hours.

Several hours later he was standing on a grassy knoll overlooking the city. Below, the city was a scene of idyllic splendor, with people wandering in parks, children playing, and pleasant sounds coming from the city. It was a gentle, passive scene. Cubal found himself troubled. This did not appear to be a war-like race. There was none of the bustle of soldiers, none of the industry necessary for weaponry, and he'd not sensed any hostility emanating from the city. He'd been in too many places where there were Crs'tings, and the manifestation of hostility was strong. Here, there was none.

He looked at the leader of the soldiers, a man named Kralt, and said, "What is the plan here?"

The man was a tall, lean individual, his face covered with a close-cropped black beard, with eyes to match. He stared hard at Cubal and replied, "We will wait until the darkness comes, then we will go in and take the city."

"What do you mean by that?"

The other glared at Cubal, his distaste for the warrior clear. He did not like this interloper, this man who seemed to be independent of rule. This was his mission, and he did not like someone who had no duties and dared question him.

"Exactly that! We take the city. We gain control."

"And how will you do that?" Cubal's voice was calm, matter-of-fact.

Kralt took a deep breath, his patience wearing thin. If it were not for the obvious favor this stranger had with Lucien, he would have killed this fool and called him a casualty of the invasion.

"We go in and destroy the three large buildings near the square. Then, we take the police compound by waiting for them to run to the scene of the explosions. As they come out, we kill them. Once we gain control of the compound, we will control the city for all of the systems run through that compound." He stepped back, one hand on his hip. "Does that explain it for you sufficiently?"

Cubal nodded. He did not reply. This plan was not to his liking, and he knew he would not be taking part in the invasion.

"I will investigate, first."

"Good. Report to me on your return." His words were crisp and commanding. Kralt wanted Cubal to know who was in charge of the mission.

"I will return, and speak with you then." With that, Cubal slipped away and headed down into the city. Within a few minutes he was standing beside a building. People walked past him. A few glanced at him and smiled, others ignored him. Children ran and played nearby.

*These are not Crs'tings.* He knew these were humans, all of them, and in some of them he detected the same aura he'd sensed in Blythe and Nathan.

He returned to where Kralt and the other soldiers stood waiting.

Cubal looked at the man, and in a tone that implied he was merely curious about the mission, asked, "What will you do once you take the city?"

The other turned from his gaze down into the city and looked back at Cubal. His face broke into a large grin, his gleaming white teeth glistening in the sun. "What we always do, of course. We eliminate everyone except the strongest of males. They are good for labor. And, a few of the children we are to save alive. Lucien continues his experiments, you know."

*Experiments? Lucien experiments on children? He murders their parents and experiments on the children?* His thoughts came like laser bullets, crashing through the images that had been erected in his mind of Lucien.

*This man is indeed a pretender. He is an evil force, as was told me.*

Cubal stood silent, looking at the man, realizing the magnitude of what he'd just heard. This man intended to exterminate an entire city. And, he expected Cubal to participate in that murderous assault. Lucien actually expected him to kill these people. It was a difficult thing for him to imagine, for in his conversations with the man, he'd not detected such a murderous disposition. He'd sensed the enormous power of the man in the beginning, but nothing that suggested this.

*Perhaps he is this evil one Blythe spoke about.*

He felt foolish. He remembered the warnings, each of them. The first warning had been the clouds with the deadly poison in them. Lucien was a cloud full of poison, of hatred that apparently ran so deep, it would scour the Earth of all humans who he did not count as loyal to him.

The second warning was of accepting what he saw, what his senses told him through the eyes, and to beware of those who bid him come to them.

*This is a test. Lucien wishes to see my reaction. If I betray him, he will come to me, pleasant and smiling, but with death in his heart.*

Cubal smiled. He felt himself falling into the warrior mode, his senses coming alive. He looked forward to the meeting.

He turned to Kralt and said in a voice that had risen now to command level, penetrating the mind with its coldness: "You will return to Lucien, now."

Kralt whirled around to face Cubal, his eyes wide with shock. Cubal knew the man's mind was panic-stricken, for his words had been forceful. The man stammered, "What...who, what is this you speak of, man?"

"You heard my command. You will take your soldiers and return to Lucien. Tell him I await his arrival."

Kralt brought his weapon around, and Cubal sensed the preparatory moves of the man and his soldiers. He said sharply: "Cease, or you will all die. I am Cubal, Wearer of the Black, and now the Gold. You will surely die if you continue."

The words brought them to an attentive state. They all knew the tales of old of such warriors. If what this one said was true, and Kralt knew deep down inside it was true, then to attempt to kill this warrior would result in instant death. He relaxed his grip on his weapon, looked back at his men and said, "Stop."

He turned back to Cubal and said carefully, not wishing to anger the warrior, "I will deliver your message." Then he smiled and added, "But, you do not understand against whom you have set yourself."

Cubal stared hard at the man and said, "You waste my time. Go."

The men turned, and in a few minutes were back in their vessel which quickly disappeared into the sky. Cubal moved away from the hill and back toward the foothills to the east. He knew Lucien would come from that direction. Whatever death he carried would be hidden and would be designed to instantly incapacitate him. Cubal wanted terrain that would help him. He raced along the short valley toward the foothills where he'd seen outcrops of granite and huge boulders lying scattered near the edges of the foothills.

He reached a large boulder and waited. It was not a long wait.

Lucien came in an unexpected fashion. Cubal had expected the man to either come in a ship, or to land at some distance and come walking over the hill toward him. Instead, the man appeared instantly before him, several yards distant. A smile was on his face.

"Greetings, my friend. I believe we have had a misunderstanding. It was never my orders nor intentions to kill anyone there. That was something Kralt said because I told him you would ask him certain questions, and he was to say exactly what he said. I wanted to test you."

*He is good. Very good. Never have I met a more capable liar.* Lucien's words were sincere, his tonal patterns perfectly pitched for sincerity, his eye movements and every muscle in his face acting in perfect accord with one telling the truth and radiating sincerity.

Cubal was impressed. He'd studied for years, the detection of those who lie. Different species give different signals, but virtually every one of them displayed some tell-tale signs of their deception. He'd never met someone he could not detect in a deception, assuming they were close enough for him to see their face, look into their eyes, or hear their voices. Even the voice can be a signal to deception.

But Lucien was perfect in every area.

Cubal permitted a slight lift of one corner of his mouth, not exactly a smile, but more of a signal to the other. He wanted Lucien to interpret it as a hesitation in his acceptance of Lucien's story. He knew the other would have known of Cubal's ability to detect deception in another, and knew his own performance had been perfect. He was not sure how Lucien would expect him to react.

*Does he know I am his enemy?* Cubal doubted that. He was certain that Lucien was still going to attempt to persuade him, to somehow gain his loyalty.

Lucien moved closer. "You have passed my test. If you had acted any other way, it would have meant that you had been subverted somewhere in your history, and I could not have trusted you. I do not want a rogue warrior out of control on my missions."

Cubal permitted the beginning of the smile to widen.

"I am sure of that," he said.

Lucien extended his hand in friendship. *Very wise move. This will tell him where I stand. I cannot permit him to touch me.* Cubal did not extend his hand.

Lucien stopped and his face underwent a sudden transformation. He was no longer the kind-looking, gentle, entreating friend, but his features were darkened, and his eyes were malevolent, the lips compressed. He spoke, and it was with a level of intensity Cubal could not imagine could ever come from another. It was akin to the level of the words Blythe had spoken, but very different. They were filled with an intense rage, filled with raw emotion and dark energies.

"You fool! Bow yourself before me, else you shall surely die, and all your warrior powers will not save you!"

Cubal felt the power driving the words as they swirled against his mind and body. But, he'd learned something about such power-speaking during the time he'd heard Blythe, and his mind and body was already on that level of focus that scattered the words from his person.

He replied, "I know not what sort of being you are, Lucien, whether man, or devil, or sorcerer, but no matter what you are, know this: Cubal, Wearer of the Gold, bows before no one, neither god nor devil!"

Suddenly, there fell upon Cubal a weight that drove him to the ground. Any other mortal would have died, but Cubal, the instant he felt the weight pressing him down, was already in action, and quickly enveloped himself in the cloak. The weight disappeared. Instantly, he shifted dimensionally to a location just behind a pre-selected boulder, and quickly tested to see if the gravity field was gone. It was. He reversed the cloak for invisibility, placed it over himself and moved away from Lucien, intending to circle around.

Suddenly, a blow stuck him, and he was hurled nearly fifty feet. He rolled, and as he regained his footing, he saw Lucien standing on a boulder, hands on his hips, laughing.

"Do you think that you can hide from me? Do you think that you, a mere mortal, can engage me in battle and win?" The laughter was shrill and piercing, and following quickly on the heels of the laughter, another blow struck Cubal. He could not see anyone, and while the blows hurt, they did not damage him. He blended his energies with the force again as it struck, and was driven nearly one hundred feet this time.

He rolled to a standing position, but this time, he spoke a single word: "Cover!" Instantly, the shield wrapped him. He stood waiting for Lucien to move against him. It would do no good to battle this one using the cloak to hide himself. Somehow Lucien could see him.

Suddenly, a great shower of sparks erupted just beneath his chin and something incredibly powerful struck the shield. Its force drove him backward a few steps. He heard a shout of astonishment and rage sound from somewhere ahead of him. But, he was moving now. He knew whatever weapon Lucien had used against him would not penetrate the shield, and that was what he wanted to know. He rushed toward the place where he'd heard the sounds, then just moments before he was there, he shifted ahead.

Behind him, another explosion, this time from a boulder that was behind his position just before the shift. *He's incredible. No one could have anticipated my maneuver.* But for the shift, that blast would have hit him.

Cubal found himself just three feet behind Lucien, who instantly whirled around. Cubal was already striking, already moving faster than the human eye could follow.

But he struck nothing. Lucien vanished.

Suddenly, he felt tremendous energies swirling in the air above him. There was a conflict of some sort going on, for he could feel the surges, and knew instantly that something unseen was happening just above him and to one side. Moreover, whatever was happening was violent, because there suddenly an explosive surge of energy above him. He moved quickly to one side. In less than a minute, there was complete calm, and he felt the tension drain from him. A calm and peace settled over him.

Cubal released the shield and looked around. There was no evidence of the presence of Lucien or any other beings.

*Why did he leave? What battle was fought and by whom?* He knew for sure that some unseen beings had engaged in a battle of some sort. And, it followed that the battle had involved Lucien, since he was gone. Cubal also knew now that whatever else Lucien might be, he was not human, or if he were, he was on a level of humanity that Cubal had never encountered. He was the exact opposite of Blythe and his family.

Cubal also knew that this was not a being whom he would be able to slay in combat, at least not unless he learned of a weakness. Thus far, he'd detected no weakness in the being that would be sufficient for Cubal to take the life force of the one called Lucien. This being had powers he'd never encountered in another being, except perhaps with Blythe.

And yet, he had been able to get close to Lucien without him being aware until the last second. He did not think he could have gotten that close to Blythe or Nathan without them being aware of his presence.

*This being has weakness. I must learn more.*

*I must leave Earth. This being will slay me if I remain. I must learn his weakness and discovery how to bring death to this strange being. To remain here in ignorance is to die.*

The thoughts brought immediate resolve. He had to find a portal of escape.

# Chapter 13

*"The voice can carry energy in its words, and properly used, can bring hesitation that is fatal. Words can also bring wisdom to the warrior who can understand their true meanings." D'VRU, BOOK ONE: The Senses*

Cubal made his way toward the city that had been marked for destruction by Lucien. There, he would inquire as to any ships leaving, or any other means of transport off the planet. He would love to have one of the A'rkji devices now, for that would be the perfect means of leaving. He knew that to remain on Earth would be to die, for in spite of his speed, and in spite of the shifting, Lucien had been but one step behind. Eventually, he'd have caught up with him, and Cubal knew from the sense of power emanating from the man on the first day of their meeting, Lucien would be able to counter any blows or efforts to slay him. Cubal did not know how long he would be able to keep Lucien from killing him, though.

The shield had held, but Cubal understood that the shield, the cloak, and his ability to do a short shift, was not sufficient, particularly if they employed the gravity weapon and the weapon of cold. If he was hit with either of those weapons during a shift or immediately upon coming out, he was doomed. And, Lucien would eventually do that. That dark being had anticipated his moves precisely, and had somehow managed to vanish before he could be harmed by Cubal. Anyone who could do that could elude death at the hands of Cubal, and could instead, bring death to the warrior.

He spotted a small building that appeared to serve food and entered. Light shone in the room from open ceilings. He recognized the P'lator Shield mechanism on the wall. It maintained a ceiling protecting against the elements, but permitted light and air to enter. The room was cool, and the sunshine lit the room with a golden brilliance. His robe played off the light and sent an array of javelin-like lances of pure gold light around the room.

From a small shielded room came an old man clothed in a white robe, with a small hood on the back. It appeared to resemble robes he'd seen in religious depictions of ancient times. The man stopped a few feet distant from him and said, "Welcome, Cubal, Wearer of the Gold." You are in the home of Justin. I greet you in the name of our Lord, Jesus Christ."

Cubal's surprise was not evident, but the man's identification of him did surprise him. It put him on alert. He was known. Apparently someone had been tracking him.

The man smiled at him and said, "Cubal, others have told me that you would be arriving. I have a message for you. Come with me." Justin turned and disappeared into a larger room, also a shielded room. Cubal followed. In the center of the room was a large array of fruits, including dates and honey, with a small basket of shelled nuts. A crystal of water was at one side of the table with a glass.

The old man poured water from the crystal into the glass, then motioned for him to come and sit at the table.

"This is prepared especially for you. I am to tell you that you need not fear. Lucien cannot harm you here. You are safe for now. Please eat. And while you eat, I have something else for you."

Justin walked to a small table, bent over it, his back to Cubal, then returned. In his hands was a book. It was a book written in the ancient form, on paper, bound between dark red coverlets, with golden edges. In dark red letters, he read Holy Bible on the cover. In terms of value, Cubal knew any collector would pay a fortune for the book.

"You were led to believe that this book was merely a fragment of a part of history, and you were trained using the *Composite Book of the Universe* in your studies, which contained bits and pieces of this book." The old man laid the book on the table near the water. "This is the entire book. You must read it, for within its pages, you will discover the answers to many mysteries that you have struggled to understand, especially as to the one you call Lucien. But, you will not understand all you read. It is not possible for you to understand some things at this time, for the true meanings are hidden from those who choose blindness. Once you have read this book, I will speak more with you." The old man moved away slowly and disappeared into a shielded room.

Cubal pulled the book toward him, opened it and began reading as he ate. One day before, he'd have dismissed the old man's request, and though he'd have taken the book, it would have been read much later, at leisure, when he felt like reading. Now, he was eager to devour the pages for there were details in this book about Lucien, and the more knowledge he had about his enemy, the better his chances at staying alive.

Four hours later, he was re-reading the book, going slower this time, fascinated with the intricate patterns he found in the book. Most readers would not have noticed them, but one of the important parts of his training was to look for patterns, whether in a book, the actions of an enemy, or anything in life that exhibited a pattern. This book contained more patterns than Cubal had ever seen in a book.

He felt they should not have called this book Holy Bible but should have named it The Book of Patterns. There were patterns of life, patterns of judgment, patterns embedded in the history of the Jewish people and their leaders, and even patterns echoing the life of the one called the Christ, the Messiah. It was the most fascinating reading he'd ever done. But, much of it was very deep and complicated. He found mystery upon mystery, and few answers to those mysteries.

The warrior found the portions detailing the being called Satan the most fascinating. If true, this was a creature far beyond the abilities of Cubal. Yet, he was puzzled. Humans had confronted this creature in the records of this book and emerged victorious. How could that be? It seemed somehow that they drew on energies from another source, this person called God.

He'd known some creatures that fed and lived on the life substance of other creatures. But, all the ones he'd met were vile creatures, destroying their host ultimately. Here, the hosts seemed to actually grow stronger, not weaker, by the habitation of this god being who took up residence within them.

On one planet, there were creatures known as the K'tss. They were as the wind, whiffs of an almost vaporous creature that sought out life forms, entered through an open orifice, such as a nose or mouth, and once in, went immediately to the brain of the invaded creature and lived in the host, feeding off its tissue for many months until the host died.

But, this god-spirit seemed different, since it inhabited the bodies of the host, who were willing subjects, and once possessed, seemed to have a strength above their own. They would have had to rely on some other source to stand against one such as Lucien. And, if this Lucien and Lucifer, or Satan, were one and the same, and Cubal was inclined now to believe it was true, then only a superior being could stand against such a foe.

No humans he knew, including himself, were that superior. He found himself wondering how he'd escaped. Something, or someone, had intervened. He knew that much.

Cubal stopped reading and relived in his mind  the brief battle, and of the moments just before Lucien disappeared. He recalled the scenes in the book where there were discussions of battles between this being and other beings like Lucien, called angels. There was a time when a large battle was made in which this being he knew as Lucien, was thrown from what appeared to be a planet called Heaven. And, there was a time when an angel named Gabriel was apparently delayed on a mission to a human who had sent a message to his god. This Gabriel indicated that he'd been delayed by this Satan or his army.

*These angel creatures stopped  Lucien's destruction of me.*

The thought that he'd been keeping in check for so long would no longer remain bound.

*They really are creatures of another dimension.  These beings called angels exist.*

Cubal was never afraid of truth, nor of acknowledging facts that did not fit his understanding. His training as a warrior forbid such a thing since danger lay in ignorance. It could be fatal to believe something to be a fact when it was a lie, or of accepting a lie as fact. He'd resisted accepting the fact about these angel beings, but he could no longer afford to do that. He'd sensed their presence.

148

His mind raced through the possibilities existing, now that he'd accepted as fact, the existence of these beings. He concluded that although there were angels, this did not mean there was this all powerful god as Blythe and the others claimed. It meant only that there were other creatures in the universe who were different, who had special powers, and who, though he had never seen them, apparently were interested in him and his well being. Logic told him that these creatures served a master whose power had to be greater than theirs. And, since Lucien had fled the battle scene without destroying him, their power had to be greater than his, which meant this master they served was greater than Lucien.

*Such power in a single entity. Can this be so?*

Suddenly, Justin appeared. He came up to the table and seated himself near Cubal. He smiled, looked at the open book and said, "I trust you have found it a most interesting book?"

Cubal returned the smile. He felt the same sense of tranquility in this man as he had felt in Blythe. "Indeed. It is unfortunate that I was not given this book to read earlier."

"Yes, well, even so, you have read it now. I must now tell you some things from this book so that you understand the kind of war that you have entered."

The white haired man paused, folded his hands together on the top of the table, then continued, "Make no mistake, Cubal. You have entered a war. It will be a brutal war and many shall die." He paused, his pale blue eyes gazing thoughtfully at Cubal, then added, "It is a universal war fought on many levels by many beings, including what we call a spiritual level. But, it is a very necessary war."

Justin smoothed his robe on one arm and adjusted his position, moving slightly to face Cubal better. "It is also a war that you are ill equipped to wage. Oh, you have skills, and are without a doubt, a warrior without peer, but this war is beyond your abilities, alone. If you attempt to wage war on your own, you will lose. You will be hurt. Perhaps you will die."

Justin watched Cubal closely for a brief moment, as though he wanted to make sure Cubal believed him, then continued, "I know that you do not accept that our Lord and Christ is our God, or that our God has created the world, indeed, the universe and all in it. Be that as it may, know this: Our God determined that for a short time, Satan, Lucien to you, should be loosed. Satan will test the entire world, and shall bring condemnation upon the world and even in the heavens, for he shall seduce many and cause them to war against God's people." He paused, then in a voice that hinted of a deep sorrow that was submerged and kept hidden, added, "He and his armies shall even seek to wage war upon heaven itself. After that, the time of cleansing shall come."

Justin folded his arms across his chest, pausing in his speech to give time for Cubal to digest his message. He continued, "Satan cannot be slain, as you understand that term. He is not immortal, but he will exist forever. God shall soon deliver him in to a place created especially for him and his followers. It is a place from which there is no escape. There is a death of a kind which humans cannot grasp, for it is an eternal life within death. It will be a death that will be a part of the fabric of the universe itself.

"This being you know as Lucien, his followers, and those other many enemies of our Christ, shall be eternally cursed from God, for they shall ever be in this place of eternal anguish, this place of eternal death, of separation from God and all of the universe."

Cubal opened his mouth to inquire as to why this god did not simply consign them to this place now, instead of later, but the man's hand raised, and Justin rose from the table and continued speaking. "Our Lord Jesus Christ has all power. But for his power and his strength, you would not have survived Lucien's attacks.

"You were right to surmise there was a battle raging in the air above you. Michael fought against Lucien, for it was forbidden of Satan to fight against you in this manner. He does not have permission to battle you in direct combat. Michael prevailed and has driven him from you. No more shall you be visited in this manner by Lucien. He may visit you, and he will continue to war against you, but you shall not be visited by him again in the manner in which you met him this day, that is, a direct, physical confrontation. However, he will send others against you who are empowered by him and who act for him, and they shall seek your life."

Justin walked over to the edge of the table near Cubal, looked down at the upturned face of the warrior and said, "Lucien may even communicate with you. It remains your decision as to whether or not you will accept those communications. You have many battles to fight, warrior. Much will be done here on Earth, but it is necessary that you leave soon, for your work is out there for now."

He pointed to the stars, then continued speaking, his voice low and mellow. "However, as you already know, Satan's reach is far. He has flung his creatures far beyond Earth, some of whom came from here, and some of whom he has corrupted with his ways and devices. And, some he has corrupted by intermingling forbidden seed with God's creations."

Cubal interrupted, "Are the Crs'tings such beings?"

Justin nodded. "They were of old, an ancient people, of Edom came they, but now are a cursed people. God shall bring them down to judgment from their nest in the stars."

Cubal's eyes widened and he reached over to the book and dragged it close, then began flipping through the pages. His memory recalled the words of Justin, and he came to the passage in the book called Obediah. He read aloud: "Though thou exalt thyself as the eagle, and though thou set thy nest among the stars, thence will I bring thee down, saith the LORD."

He looked up at Justin and said, "These are the Crs'tings?"

Justin nodded. "They, and creatures created by Lucifer, were sent from this planet many thousands of years ago. It is generally thought that travel to the stars came with our Lord, but Lucifer knew such secrets long ago and helped the Edomites build ships that took them from Earth to another world he told them about. They began a new life there in the stars, along with the creatures that Lucifer created. From time to time, these creatures would return to Earth."

Cubal's curiosity was high. "What was their purpose?"

"They came to visit with Lucifer, but also to capture humans, animals, and other creatures from Earth for their experiments. You see, it has been Lucifer's goal to create his own race, to duplicate the work of our Lord, and to have humans that were his children, and who did not belong to the Lord."

"Has he done this?"

Justin's face was somber. He nodded. "Indeed. Lucifer has had children upon this planet for thousands of years. They appear human, but they have no spirit. Their father is Lucifer."

Cubal rose to his feet. "Have the humans mingled their seed with that of Lucien's creations?"

Justin replied. "Yes. It was for this reason that our God made great efforts to keep pure the blood line of his people. Our Lord Jesus descended from a pure bloodline, untainted by Lucifer's work."

"What differences are there in humans and those who are of Lucien, or Lucifer as you call him.?"

"It is impossible for anyone to know the difference, for they were as we were, in every way, except one: they had no spirit."

Cubal nodded slowly. "I am beginning to understand, now, why I have felt certain things about some humans I have met. There was a difference with some. It was as though they were lacking in certain energies I usually detect in humans. I thought it to be a difference that lay in the birth, where one child embraces life loudly, and another comes into life with a whimper and small sounds. I see now, I have misunderstood."

Justin said, "These beings are without true emotions. Oh, they have feelings, but all of their feelings are focused on pleasing themselves. Every human can be selfish. However, these beings can only be selfish. They can only live to please themselves. They have no conscience. A human may have a conscience that is seared, but these beings are never possessed even of a seared conscience, since they never hold one. Their father has no conscience, nor do they."

Cubal asked, "And so, the Crs'tings are created humans, made from Lucien's labs?"

Justin nodded. "Yes, though some of them are human. They are a corrupted people." He paused for a long moment, then added, "They began doing cloning experiments in order to replace humans here on earth. They even made a duplicate of yourself, as you know. They have continued with their cloning techniques since you last met them, but they are still unable to perfectly duplicate a human, since they cannot create a spirit."

Cubal abruptly changed the subject, anxious to begin his investigation into the strengths and weaknesses of his enemy. He

152

said, "I saw one of Lucien's devices in which he visits other worlds. He said he used the device to whisper to the Crs'tings and bring fear to them, which caused them to abandon their attacks on Earth and the Dominion Worlds."

Justin nodded. "Yes, he assisted in the invention of this device. But, he did not whisper to the Crs'tings. Those beings are a part of his army. He is a liar and always has been a liar. He has caused much harm with this device."

"So why doesn't your god stop his use of this device?"

Justin smiled. "The mystery of iniquity, and of this being we call Lucifer, will one day be explained to all, when time shall be no more, and when there shall be a new heaven and Earth, for this creature has corrupted the Earth and the heavens, and then there shall be no more time. That God could stop Satan's use of the device, I know. Since God has not stopped him, there is purpose in it. I do not purport to know that purpose, for God's wisdom is infinite."

Cubal looked down for he did not want to show his displeasure in the words he'd heard. It did not seem to him that a god who had all power, and who was clearly at war with another god-like creature, would permit that creature to have a weapon that enabled that one to wage war against him and his people. It was not logical. It was not the way of a warrior. It was not the way of any king he'd ever known. It was not the way to win a war. One did not give an opponent any edge, nor permit that opponent to have opportunities to hurt you. That was fundamental to a war. It was fundamental to a fight. It was essential to winning.

*This god creature does not war. He plays a game.* The thoughts were ugly and as they came, his upper lip curled in anger.

Yet, he had to acknowledge that this god, this Christ king, did have some unusual powers. He did command beings who seemed to have more power than Lucien. And that was impressive to Cubal, for he knew the power of Lucien. Moreover, if the stories in the book about this creature were true, then Lucien had even more power than he'd sensed in his first meeting with the creature.

Justin rose and said, "You should remain here for several days. Lucien will not seek you in here. It is forbidden. He still wants you for his service, but for now he has been thwarted. He thought he could trick you into doing harm to innocents, and then use your great sense of guilt to begin a searing of your conscience. You would do anything to forget, and he would have shown you ways to forget. Lucien had a drug prepared especially for you. It was not the life drug. It was a drug that would have altered you in ways you cannot imagine, for it was constructed especially for you."

"Why did he send me on a mission before he gave me the drug? It would have made more sense, would it not, to have given me the drug?"

Justin smiled. "His arrogance caused him to believe that you were in his power, and even if you attempted to escape, he was not worried. He felt he could transport you to his complex and administer the drug against your will."

He paused, then continued, "He was not prepared for the powers of the cloak and shield, nor for your shifting ability. That surprised him. And, although he knew Michael would appear, he felt he would be able to overwhelm you before Michael could arrive." The man's smile widened and he added, "Once again, he has underestimated the power of our God, and he underestimated you and your powers."

The man put his hands into the large sleeves, the left hand in the right sleeve and the right hand in the left sleeve and moved backward a few steps. In a lowered voice that was almost servile, he said, "I am told to assist you in any way you wish, including providing you with a means for escape from Earth, if that is what you wish."

"I wish to meet with your god."

Justin's eyebrows furrowed and his eyes narrowed as he stared for a long moment at Cubal, clearly surprised at the response. "That will come in time."

"You said you could assist me. I wish to meet with your god."

Justin smiled. "It is not so simple as that, Cubal. It is written that no man may see God and live."

"Did not those who were called disciples see your Christ and live? And, did not you and others like you, live during his rule here on Earth, and view him, and yet live? Why then, do you say I cannot see this god who wishes me to wage war on his behalf?"

"Your logic is as sharp as a Synthian's blade. You will see God one day. However, I must tell you that while this meeting shall one day occur, it will come not at your demand, but will come at the time and choosing of our God. One does not summon God to a meeting. He is as the wind, going where he will, at times gentle, at times boisterous, invisible to all, but visible in effect. Further, you must continue to read the book I gave you, for therein are instructions that will give you the meeting you desire. As it is written, if one draws nigh to God, then God will draw nigh to him. And again, it is written that we are to seek the Lord whilst he may be found."

Cubal sighed. The religious speech was expected, yet he'd hoped for more. He'd hoped for more direct talk and had hoped to meet this being and discuss battle plans with him. He was troubled that there were apparently expectations to use him in battle, but that he could not meet with the one who was apparently in charge of the war. It was not the way war was conducted. Plans had to be made. Strategies had to be discussed and developed. Armies had to be raised. Enemy strength had to be evaluated. Attack points had to be ascertained. So many things went into waging war. It was a complicated process, one he'd been trained for since birth, and one which he knew better than any human ever born.

*And I cannot meet with the one in charge of this war.*

Cubal stood and extended his hand. "You have been kind to me, Justin. I must say I hear your words and accept that you are a sincere person, and a good man. This I know, for you are as another I have known called Blythe. I do not understand all about such beings as yourselves. You are not entirely human, as I have known humans. Your flesh is different from mine, this I can tell, and you have not the same aura as other humans I have known. There is a different, ah...you would call it spirit, yes, a different spirit within such beings as yourselves. And, I know that you are indestructible, at least from one such as me."

Justin smiled and took Cubal's hand. "Blythe is a fine man. He is a friend, and has spoken highly of you. And, it is true that we are different from such as yourself. You have flesh and blood. We are of a resurrected body, a spiritual body and mind  not subject to the physics of your world, but only subject to the will of our God. And, the different spirit—and you were right to call it that—is indeed different, for our spirit is God's spirit. We are one with God, and what you see is but a manifestation of our God through these bodies and minds. He has chosen to speak to you in this fashion, through messengers such as ourselves. And so it was before our time. God sent messengers to his people, to speak to them, to warn them, to help them, to deliver them, and sometimes to punish them."

"So I have read."

Justin said, "Cubal, you must tell me what you wish to do."

Cubal smiled at the other and said, "What is it that your god and my apparent general, or king, or whatever title it is that he takes, desires?"

The old man laughed, his laughter a light, airy laugh of genuine mirth. His eyes crinkled up and his face was broken in a broad grin. "You are delightful! Blythe said you would surprise me. I did not expect such an answer."

"My skepticism has misled you. Although I do not worship the one you call god, for I acknowledge no gods nor devils, but only superior beings of one kind or another, with powers of one kind or another, I also recognize that we are on the same side in this war. I do know that this being called Lucien, whom you call Satan, is evil. He must be stopped, for he will seek to destroy many humans, and this I cannot permit while I draw breath. Thus, I will align myself to the enemies of Lucien, whomever they are, regardless of the gods they serve or do not serve."

Cubal paused and with a slight smile added, "This does not mean I believe the story about your god who came from a world called Heaven—though I accept this man may have come from a planet you call Heaven—and that this one called Jesus hung on a piece of wood, became guilty of all the evils of mankind, died, then rose again the third day, came back here and ruled for a thousand years, and is now returned to his heaven world; and further, that this man-god is now engaged in a war with Lucien and others called devils." His words came in a rush, almost a mocking chant. "I cannot believe all that, Justin, though I do believe your god is in a war with Lucien."

Justin replied, "You shall one day see the power of our Lord for he shall destroy all enemies of God and of mankind."

Cubal lost his smile and he said softly, "I can accept that your king, the one you call Christ, will one day imprison Lucien, perhaps

156

for as long as this being is capable of living. But Justin, convey to your master that although I will serve him in this war, I will not bow before him, nor will I ever worship him."

Justin nodded. "I understand. I once was almost as you, an agnostic, actually. I did not know whether there was a god or not, and did not really care, frankly. You are perhaps the truest atheist I have ever met. And, your reasoning, though flawed, is measured and practical."

Cubal chuckled. "Tell me, Justin, the one who does not project an aura of being so old as he appears, what piece of evidence, what vision, what event caused you to change your mind and believe in the god status of this Jesus person?"

Justin's eyebrows raised. "You are indeed a curious one, as Blythe said you were. Again, you have surprised me. You appear to reject the notion of God being the Lord of all creation, yet you have a curiosity that drives you to learn more." He stepped away from Cubal and walked to the end of the table, stopped, then turned back to Cubal, resting one hand on the table.

"I was not a nice man, evil in my ways, hating without cause, and hurting without provocation. In me dwelt what is explained so eloquently by the Apostle Paul as sin."

Cubal interrupted with a smile on his face. "Yes, that would be in the section labeled Romans, would it not?"

Justin nodded. "Yes. You have remembered correctly." He placed his hands behind his back and began walking towards the window, as he continued his story. "One day I met a man who called himself a Christian. We talked of many things, and inevitably, the conversation turned to speaking about God. I did not do as so many do, that is, hush him, for I did not, as many did, fear discussions of God. I did not fear whatever he might say to me because I actually enjoyed the dialog.

"But, it happened one day that I was in his home that he had left quite a large sum of money out on a table much like this one. I stole that money. When I saw him again, several days later, I realized that he knew I'd taken his money. I was prepared for my defense, namely that I had been deeply in debt to the Lenders, and they were going to kill me. I counted on his forgiveness. But, he did not mention it and was as kind to me as if I were a son."

Justin circled the table, warming to his opportunity to tell his story. "Over several months, we continued to speak, and because of the guilt I had, I suppose I listened a little more than I might have otherwise listened, though at times, when I tired of his conversation about God, I would interrupt him and turn the conversation into a direction that was less boring.

"One particular day, this man began reading from the same book you have there. He read the following words: 'And I saw a great white throne, and him that sat on it, from whose face the earth and the heaven fled away; and there was found no place for them. And I saw the dead, small and great, stand before God; and the books were opened: and another book was opened, which is the book of life: and the dead were judged out of those things which were written in the books, according to their works. And the sea gave up the dead which were in it; and death and hell delivered up the dead which were in them: and they were judged every man according to their works. And death and hell were cast into the lake of fire. This is the second death. And whosoever was not found written in the book of life was cast into the lake of fire.'

"Immediately, I felt a strong sense of truth, as though I knew absolutely that what I'd just heard was true. I could not get away from the image that sprang to my mind of this white throne and this being from whom the earth and heavens fled. And then came the knowledge that I would be judged for my evil. I began to feel very guilty about my theft. The wrong I'd done to him shone like a brilliant light inside me, giving me extreme discomfort. But, I held it in check."

Justin walked away from Cubal a short distance, turned back to the warrior, then continued. "My friend continued to read from the Book. He read to me where it says 'For all have sinned and come short of the glory of God.' He explained to me that everyone, himself included, had sinned, had done wrong, and everyone, including himself, was guilty before God. I resisted his words."

Justin reached over, patted the open Bible, and continued, "For several sessions, he would read things from this book to me. He spoke of this God coming down from Heaven and taking on the form of a man, but without the evil typical of man, for he was born of a virgin and holy in all that he did. He told me that God had what some would call a code of justice, and that in his view, all of his creation had violated that code, had sinned, and that he had judged them all worthy of destruction.

"Then, my friend told me that God decided to do something remarkable. He actually became human. He did this because some human was required to accept the penalty that he had decreed, for all of humanity. You know the story that was told in the Bible about Jesus being crucified. That was our God, in human form, not merely accepting death as a human, but being found guilty of the sins of humans.

"It really came to me then. I understood. I had been judged and found guilty, but this man called Jesus—Messiah we call him— became guilty of all my sin, just as though he'd actually did those things. He became guilty, before the Father, of my theft. I began to hear its message for the first time."

Justin paused as he recalled the events, then continued. "It was an incredible thought to me, to consider that the God who created the entire universe, this same God would take upon himself the limitations of a human, come to this planet in human form, his vast powers laid aside, all for the sole purpose of being beaten and hung on a cross, and declared guilty of the wickedness of many.

"One day, I could no longer resist its power. I knelt with this man, and for the first time in my life, acknowledged the existence of God and of Messiah, God's sacrifice for all of mankind. It was at this time that I knew I could no longer live as I had lived, but that my life had to change. It had to be a life lived for my God. So, I asked my friend to forgive me, and asked God to forgive me. I apologized for my sins to God, and asked for pardon and for eternal life. When I arose, there was a great peace in my heart, but there was more than that. I knew that I was different in here. I knew God was now a part of me and I was a part of God." Justin tapped a finger against his chest.

"It was not dramatic. But, it was real. The guilt was gone, and I knew that I was forgiven by God, that the sacrifice by Jesus Christ for my sins had been sufficient. And, I knew that the Spirit of the living God somehow had actually entered my body and now possessed me."

Justin stood now silent, smiling at Cubal.

The warrior was solemn as he replied. "Justin, please understand that although I do not question your sincerity, I must question the interpretation of it all. It is all, for me, very improbable, and I have lived all my life evaluating probabilities. I measure life in many ways. Realize that I have never one time been sorrowful for anything I have done. I have regretted some choices that were tactical in character, that is, in choices of weapons, or strategy, but not of moral actions I have taken.

"I do not see myself as what you term a sinner. Frankly, I do not understand that term. I have precepts that I have been taught and which I accepted long ago that have placed me on a level of conduct that is far above the conduct of the ordinary human. There are no vices permitted to such a one as myself. I am celibate and have long since controlled my needs for women. I eat carefully. I do not seek the harm of others unless they seek my harm, or the harm of those I protect or defend."

Justin nodded. "I understand, Cubal. You are indeed a unique individual, more different than any I have ever met. I can understand why it is that you would find it difficult to accept the idea of sin, or the need for repentance and sorrow for that sin, or even the concept of God. But, I am not the one, ultimately, to persuade you. That remains for God, not Justin. I am merely a messenger of God's truth."

He turned then and moved toward the shielded entry to his room. "Continue your stay here, and when you have decided what you wish to do, let me know. Also, if you wish to dialog further, I am at your service."

"But, I have already told you, what is it that your god wishes? After all, it is his war, is it not?"

Justin smiled. "God wishes for you to decide what it is that you wish to do, and then for me to assist you as I am permitted in carrying that task out." He paused, then added, "That plan does not include an assault on Lucien's dwelling. If that is your thought, then please change your mind, for it is too soon and you would perish there."

"But would not my general send Michael to rescue me? A slight grin crossed Cubal's face and quickly faded.

Justin shook his head slowly, suppressed outright laughter, and instead, smiled, then disappeared into another room.

# Chapter 14

*"It has been said that wars are fought by men and decided by the gods. The true warrior shall enter each battle believing his actions will decide the war."* D'VRU, BOOK FIVE: The Unseen

Cubal's choice was not one which he would have ordinarily chosen. Normally, he would have chosen to leave immediately in order to secure his person, and to determine what weapon or weapons or strategies were necessary in order to resist, defend and attack Lucien successfully.

But, there was one thing he had to know before he left. He had to test one thing told him by Justin. He'd said Lucien would not come against him as he had before. If that were true, he had to know it, for if true, then perhaps he could remain longer on Earth. Lucien would send others, but did they have the power of Lucien? He doubted it. That being's nature was not such that he would share all of his power with another. He might lend some of his power to another, and he might work on behalf of another, but there would not be another person using the full powers of Lucien against him.

Justin had spoken as if this were an established fact. If true, it would tell him much about the nature of the war, for it would mean that there was indeed some entity who could command this being. In other words, there were some rules to this war, and Lucien was forced to abide by those rules. Cubal was willing to put himself at risk to gain this information.

Justin did not act surprised when Cubal said he was going to leave the city, and requested a small vessel in which to move about. The vessel was provided, and Cubal left after informing Justin that he was going to the city of the Angels on the coast of that part of the world formerly called America. There, he would live for a time quietly, studying the people and their ways, and learning what he could about Lucien's forces. Justin did not comment, but merely bid him a "Godspeed," and a short handshake.

It took Cubal but minutes to reach the city. Once there, he obtained living quarters high in one of the anti-grav living units. He could stand on his balcony, hundreds of feet in the air, and see much of the city and the surrounding mountains. He knew from ancient pictures that the terrain around the city was completely different now. Before, the old city stood near the ocean. Now, many lakes surrounded the city and islands dotted the coast. The old city was deep beneath the waves of the ocean.

That afternoon, he took a passenger flyer to the ground and began his exploration of the city. He walked with the wariness of a soldier entering a hot zone, knowing enemies were around, never knowing exactly where, never knowing their true strength, but he also walked as a warrior, a disciple of D'vru, fearless, and completely confident in his abilities to counter any attacks by such enemies.

The city was obviously deteriorating. He saw roads that were in need of repair, weeds growing across paths, and buildings that were weathered and cracking. Trash could be seen near the sides of many of the buildings. A wide road wound past one building, and as he glanced down the road, he could see that it led to a section of the city he'd noticed from above that appeared to have less air activity and more ground activity.

He walked slowly down the path beside the road, overgrown with weeds, and as he continued, he noticed that the trash was in greater abundance. Ground vehicles moved down the road at great speed. Crowds were gathered in some spots, some talking, some merely standing and watching. Brilliant in-depth image scenes washed across the sides of buildings advertising goods or displaying messages.

He stopped and listened to one individual as he spoke. The man was dressed in the brown casual garb worn by those who conveyed the world news events, called Resonators. His hair was long, flowing over his shoulders. His voice was deep and melodic, a powerful magnet to the listener.

"And you all know that this man has done more to assist our world in the transition period than any others. There are many who, once the iron rule of the prior king left, decided to be king themselves. They would enslave you. Those who are in the city where once the government issued its iron edicts, have attempted to continue their harsh religious rule over us. Lucien will stop them in their quest!"

The mention of Lucien brought Cubal to a stop. He stood and listened longer, hearing a lengthy speech about the evils brought upon the world by the long reign of the Christ king and how all of them had to be stopped. It was powerful rhetoric.

*You lie, as does your commander.* A smile lifted one corner of his mouth as the thought came.

He continued his journey. After nearly a mile, he found himself in a part of the city that had clearly been neglected even more than others. City services were not here. Refuse was everywhere. The people were in unshielded homes, some of the homes badly damaged from some kind of assault by weapons. The crowds were larger here, people wandering slowly, as though they had somewhere to go but were in no hurry to get there. Others merely stood around staring into the distance.

As he passed by one small group, a man called out to him, "Sir, have you any food?"

Cubal stopped and looked at a short man, balding, clad in a short cloak , wearing pants of a dirty linen of the old style cloth goods. He replied, "I have no food, sir. But, why is it that you have no food? Is not this the planet of plenty? It is so known in the universe."

The man shook his head slowly. "No longer. We suffer much, now that our Lord has left."

"You mean the Christ?"

"Yes. When he was here, such things as you see would not be permitted."

Suddenly, a loud voice sounded: "Yoder! Still your blasphemous mouth! You will be punished for your foolish words." A large man, clad in a blue-green uniform of the city's police force stepped from behind a shielded door. He walked over to the man called Yoder, and without warning, kicked the man in the chest. Yoder flew backward, landing in the dirt. The big man followed after the fallen man.

When he reached Yoder, he found Cubal standing just in front of the man. It startled the policeman and he reacted by leaping backward.

"What? Who are you? Stand clear of this man!" he demanded.

"You will not harm this man." Cubal's voice was low, but he projected as much menace in his voice as he could. The other stepped back another few feet, clearly impacted by the words.

The man shook his head as if to clear the words from his mind, then said, "If you do not remove yourself, we will take you into headquarters and there expose you to the Interrogator."

Cubal's interest was aroused. "Then you shall take me to such person, for I will not stand aside." Immediately, he knelt beside the man called Yoder and whispered, "As soon as they attack me, you must run from here. Find another place to live, for they will seek to destroy your life after today." Yoder nodded, tears in his eyes from the fear.

Cubal stood and advanced on the policeman. Suddenly, a trio emerged from the same shielded door and advanced upon Cubal. Each held a small laser pistol. Cubal was concerned that one of them would fire, which would cause him to have to betray himself to them. He was in no hurry to do that because he wanted them to take him to the Interrogator. He spoke softly, and his shield enveloped his body. He advanced toward the policemen.

Suddenly, one fired at him. The showers from the explosion against the shield scattered, blinding anyone who'd been looking at Cubal. The warrior leaped backward, scooped up the man called Yoder and raced several feet away, around the edge of a building. He deposited the man on the ground and said, "You must flee." The man's eyes widened and without a word, he raced away.

Cubal stepped from behind the building, his hands raised in the universal sign of surrender.

"I will go willingly with you to your Interrogator."

The policemen surrounded him. One of them grabbed him roughly by the shoulders and attempted to press him to the ground but suddenly, inexplicably, discovered himself lying on the ground, his right arm numb with pain. Another grabbed Cubal, only to discover that his hand suddenly developed a severe cramp that shot all the way up to his shoulder.

Cubal stopped them with a raised hand. "I will go with you, but you cannot touch my person. I will not permit that. If you attempt to hurt me, stun me, or in any way subdue me, I will not permit this."

The police squad stood there for a long moment. They'd already seen this man do things that they could not understand, and fear was upon them. Finally, the original policeman who'd kicked the man called Yoder said, "It is well enough. We will escort."

"You lead. I will follow. Do not come behind me."

The squad led Cubal down what appeared to be a small side street to a large shielded building. It's front was a brilliant blue, outlined with white. As they walked through the shield, Cubal felt the energies of a probe and knew his body was being scanned for weapons and identity.

"Welcome, Cubal, to the Interrogator. You will be seated." The voice was cloned, a digital rendition without emotion.

Cubal ignored the policeman's pointed finger showing him the chair in which he was to sit. Instead, he stood just outside the circle that he'd recognized as the zone for a transport device. Before he was transported anywhere, he wanted to know where. It would not have surprised him to find himself transported directly to Lucien's headquarters.

"Where is this transporter set to send me?"

"What do you mean?" The big policeman on his left acted innocent.

"I know what this device is and want only to know its setting. I may permit you to transport me, if I like the setting."

He heard a muffled laugh, then, "It is set for a beautiful beach where there are beautiful women, and you may stay as long as you like." The laughter was less muffled now.

Cubal ignored the policemen and moved quickly to the small room just off to one side. He entered the room and saw a little man also clad in a police uniform sitting at a huge console. The man's eyes widened as he saw the warrior's entrance. His mouth opened to speak, but Cubal raised his hand for silence.

"I only want to know where this thing is set to transport. Do not lie to me or I will toss you into the circle, and you shall go there, instead." He paused for effect and his eyes locked into the others' as he added, "Do you believe me?"

The man nodded and glanced over Cubal's shoulder where the other policemen had appeared. Cubal turned to them and said, "Leave or die." His voice carried his words in commanding tones and the threat was obvious.

The policemen backed slowly away from the door. Cubal turned to the other and said, "Will you tell me or do I toss you onto the transport?"

The man swallowed hard and said, "It is to the slave ship Bvsenium."

"And where does the slave ship Bvsenium go?"

The man wiped his face as sweat droplets appeared on his forehead. "I do not know. They are always there."

*A transport ship that will shuttle the slaves to another ship or planet.*

"Tell me, little one, and if you lie, I will place you on the circle, tell me who it is that you send to this ship?"

"What do you mean?"

"I mean who do the policemen have orders to send to the ship?"

The man was silent for a long time but the sight of the warrior standing there so menacingly was too much. His resistance broke completely. "We send only those who will not renounce allegiance to our former king."

"And on whose orders?"

"Lucien's soldiers."

"How long has this been in place?"

"I do not know for certain. It was here when I came, and I have been here one year."

"Very well." He turned away from the man, and just before he exited, he stopped, turned to the man and said, "I am going to stand in the circle. I am very fast and I believe I can get out of the circle before you can press that red transport button. Would you like to see if I am that fast? I can move as fast as the light. There is no one faster than me." Cubal knew the man probably thought he was insane, and he could see the eagerness wash over the man's swarthy features.

"Yes, I would like to see such a thing!" he said, the excitement raising his voice to a treble.

"All right, I will go and stand there, and when I say the word "ready,' you will press the transport button, and I will attempt to escape. Is that fair?"

The other gulped, hardly able to believe his good fortune and grinning at the prospect of pressing the button before the fool could speak. He only wished he could see the man's surprise when he realized he'd been tricked. He would have a few years to think about it on whatever planet or mining asteroid he arrived.

Cubal entered the circle and said loudly, "All right, I'm here...." Instantly, he vanished, and did not see the little man standing at the panel, his finger on the transport button, a look of absolute glee on his face.

But, he did see the squadron of soldiers who stood, weapons at the ready and pointed at him, as he materialized aboard the ship. They grabbed him roughly and shoved him forward to a circle similar to the one he'd just left. Without warning, Cubal erupted into a flurry of violence. Soldiers were hurled about the ship, weapons went flying, and men were staggering, then falling to the floor. Cubal swept through the small force of soldiers like the wind through grass, bringing each of them to an instant state of unconsciousness. Then, he went through the entire ship until there were no more soldiers nor crew left standing. He stripped each of them of weapons and uniforms, dragged them to the transport circle that they'd tried to push him onto.

He went to the control panel and saw that the destination was set for the Pegos jungles. Those soldiers would quickly learn the fate of all those they'd sent through the portal, for the life span of one sent to the jungle was only measured in months, seldom more than a year, provided they did not perish sooner from one of the deadly creatures that lurked in the thick vegetation. He glanced at the large pile of soldiers, then pressed the transport button.

Then, he quickly flipped through the screens of location data. These were locations where there was a destination receptor. He counted nine reception points, most of them mining asteroids. Cubal worked his way through the system controls, resetting coordinates, and scanning the huge database onboard the old shuttle ship. It was a ship several hundred years in age, used in the early days to transport settlers to other worlds. It was sleek in design, with many creature comforts, soft, cushioned seats, a spacious garden eco-system near the center of the ship, and even exercise runs throughout the ship. The new owners had brought in all new equipment.

Cubal stopped when he located the Earth coordinates. He scanned slowly and discovered that there were seven receptor ports on Earth. He studied the maps that translated the coordinates. One would put him back where he came from, two others appeared to go directly to Lucien's main headquarters, two more went somewhere into the western mountainous portions identified on the screen maps as "Ancient City of North America." The other two went to locations on the other side of the world. Cubal thought for a long moment, wanting to return to the same portal just to see the surprise on the face of the policeman, but knowing that it was a foolish whim he could not afford to indulge.

Instead, curiosity bade him choose one of the ancient cities of North America. Before he left, he reset the receptor from the City of Angels so that it would automatically forward anyone sent to the ship, to the same location he was about to visit. If it was a place where Lucien had soldiers stationed, he'd return and reset the coordinates.

He activated the timer on the console, stepped onto the circle, and instantly found himself alone in a dark, unlit chamber. He remained still while his senses adjusted to his surroundings. It was a dark and damp location, and he sensed that it was raining outside. He moved slowly toward a small corridor. Moments later, he emerged into a larger room with no lighting, but which had open, unshielded sky on one entire side. An explosion of some sort had ripped away the domed ceiling there. He moved through the room slowly, investigating, looking here and there. Everything he saw showed decay and damage. There had been battles fought in this city. He saw bones, human, mingled with animal bones, wrecked vehicles, buildings with huge gaping holes in them, and everywhere, pieces of metal from homes and buildings and vehicles. This city had been ravaged.

*Lucien has stripped this city of its people.*

He knew none of those people in this city were still alive for they'd all been transported. They'd died on foreign worlds in the muck and mire of some jungle or on the frozen, harsh bleakness of some asteroid. But, at least there did not appear to be any of Lucien's solders here. This would be a good location for those kidnapped citizens. They could perhaps start life anew, here.

*This creature must be stopped.* Instantly, on the heels of the thought came another, unbidden, erupting with emotion.

*You who call yourself God! See what this one has done to your people? See the evil here! If you are truly a god, help me stop this being!*

The thoughts were packed with deep feelings of anger. Such events would not be done against a true god, or his people. His anger subsided, and a smile flitted across his face. He found it ironic that he was aligned with a god in whom he did not believe, and who he could not meet, fighting a war this god did not seem to be winning. And yet, certain things kept coming back to him, like the sudden departure of the Crs'tings. He knew it was not Lucien. That had been a lie, for this creature, and the goals of the Crs'tings, were identical. And, he recalled the fight with Lucien. That creature had been driven away from him. Cubal doubted he would have survived the encounter if it had lasted longer.

There was a mystery here that he was determined to solve.

Suddenly, he heard a whooshing sound. All around him small ships and hundreds of men in glider, anti-grav suits, all heavily armed, were descending upon the city.

*Lucien knows I am here.*

Cubal instantly went to a level five, and moved away from his location, and the three descending soldiers who were dropping near his position. He knew that Lucien would be completely aware of his capabilities and would have arranged this attack accordingly. The weaponry would be sophisticated.

That deep inner level of consciousness took over as he moved away, his senses acute. He could hear the breathing of some of the soldiers, and grunts as they shed their landers. Footsteps pounded the dirt, headed in his direction.

Ordinarily, Cubal would have moved directly into the moving force. That was the way of the warrior, for in the middle, one can spread confusion, and the attack would sow confusion and fear into the attackers. But, Lucien would know that. He would have a trap set for such an action. Instead, Cubal melted into the shadows, reversing his cloak to hide his movements. He whispered for his shielded covering.

The warrior stepped away from the building, and just as he started to move across a small, shadowy patch of ground, he stumbled, tripped by some unseen object. But, his attention was now focused on the eleven soldiers who came running around the corner of a nearby building. They stopped and began setting up what appeared to be some sort of command post. Cubal moved closer and watched intently as they established a communications link screen, and then a small portal. No doubt, the portal was to move soldiers and weaponry around the battle scene as necessary. A minute later, he'd made his way to the post, then he crept silently amongst the soldiers. In a few seconds all were lying on the ground. Not a sound had come from any of them.

Cubal removed a small, round object from his cloak, spoke softly to it, then set it within the panel of the communications device. Quickly, he flashed through the settings for the portal. It seemed that there were three locations, two just outside the city and one located in the City of Angels. Without hesitation, he set the location for the City of Angels, placed one of the soldiers on the portal entry platform, then cloaked himself to render his body invisible. Cubal picked up the limp body of the soldier and stepped through the portal.

Immediately, he found himself in a large arena of some sort. He dropped the soldier who fell to the ground. Cubal moved quickly to one side, knowing that all attention would be on the soldier. If

Lucien had anticipated his move here, and he had to expect this was something that Cubal would manage to do, then the soldier would give him the time he needed to escape.

There were nearly twenty soldiers surrounding the portal, all weapons trained on the portal. One fired, which set off the others. The soldier lying on the portal, and the portal itself, disappeared in a blur of fire and smoke. Cubal was already near the other side of the arena. He neared an exit and discovered that exit was blocked with a spidery-like force field. It appeared to be the same kind of field used by the interstellar ships to ward off meteorites, but was slightly different in both appearance and the energies it gave off.

*He anticipated my moves, again. He was hoping I did not know about shifting through this kind of field.*

He was trapped.

Lucien had correctly assumed Cubal would make it to the portal, and even assumed that he would get through the portal unscathed. Cubal knew Lucien would have been prepared at any location he would have chosen.

A loud voice sounded suddenly in the arena: "Cubal! I know you are here. By now, you know there is no escape."

*Lucien! So he does come. And it was a fool's tale that he would not confront me directly.* Anger surged through him for believing Justin, then quickly subsided. The old man wanted to believe in the great power of his god, and it was not his fault that he accepted the word of others. He'd merely told Cubal what he'd been told. His god was at fault for this.

Then, just as quickly, he knew the old man's words were true. *Lucien would have appeared by now! He has indeed somehow been stopped from coming against me directly. It was not forbideen of him to communicate with me.*

Cubal's mind was racing, recalling everything he knew and had heard about force fields. And suddenly, he knew he had an answer, a hope for escape. He was not concerned about the soldiers. He could afford to let them live, for they were not the real danger to him. He now knew that somewhere within this vast arena lay a weapon which Lucien would use against him.

But, if there was a weapon, and if Cubal could locate that weapon quickly enough, he could escape. His senses were extended, his mind free as he looked about the entire area. His eyes fell upon a small rise near one end of the arena.

*That's it. The weapon would be at an end so its controls would be accessible from outside the shield. It lies buried and will rise from that point.* Even as he thought, he was moving, running faster than he'd ever moved in his life, shielded and cloaked, but not with the invisibility. Instead, he ran cloaked against the weapons of death about which he had been told.

As he moved, the weapon rose from the hill, dirt falling from it, the hum of the energies emanating from the weapon making a low pitched groan. Cubal could hear the screams of the soldiers.

*Lucien would sacrifice an army in order to slay me.* He understood that. He would do the same, if necessary to destroy an enemy such as himself. Lives lost in the conquest of an army, or the defeat of one who has the potential of destroying you and costing you the war, were negligible. It was an acceptable loss to a true commander of armies.

Cubal did not feel the effects of the weapon and could not be sure whether it was the gravity machine or some other weapon. The screams were gone now. Then, he was at the weapon, leaping onto the back of it's huge flat, silvery surface. A short, squared barrel nearly four feet in length and the same in width, jutted from the weapon. He turned and saw a silvery landscape, a place frozen with the chill of space. It was an unsettling sight, for he knew that this weapon could and would eventually, if not already, be used upon other people, innocents who would, in the blink of an eye, be frozen solid, and some aliens who would awaken as slaves with such short lives left to live.

He crouched near the back part of the weapon, the point closest to the shield, and ran his hands quickly over the flat surface of the weapon. It was not cold.

*Good. It is as I suspected. This weapon must receive warmth, else it will become brittle.*

Cubal lowered his covering shield. Now he stood and moved forward until he was directly on top of the barrel, near the edge.

"Front!" The shield immediately sprang into place, just in front of the barrel of the weapon.

He backed up a short distance, as he saw the shield was still inches from the opening of the barrel. The shield was now covering the opening. He reached one hand down and smiled, as he felt cold seeping into the metal. In another minute, the cold in the metal was frosting the entire structure. The warming mechanism was designed for a weapon which would release its radiant cold, not trap it within itself. Then, with all the power in him, Cubal focused his mind and power, and with a massive blow of his fist that would have shattered even a Retlian's body armor, he struck the flat surface of the weapon near the shield.

Instantly, the weapon shattered. Cubal leaped as the weapon disintegrated, and his body went hurtling toward the opening created by the weapon. He tumbled through the empty place in the shield and as he rolled, he shifted. In seconds, he shifted again, moving through the night as a phantom, never stopping more than a second.

# Chapter 15

*"The perception of your opponent is a weapon at your disposal. Use it wisely and discretely, but never openly."*
*D'VRU, BOOK FIVE: The Unseen*

Early morning brought him to the door of Justin. The old man greeted him as though he'd been gone to visit a friend for a few minutes, then ushered him into the same room with the same table. A basket of fruit and nuts with water was on the table, as before.

"Come and rest. You must nourish your body. It has been a very strenuous time for you."

Cubal raised his eyebrows and smiled at the other. "Justin, you are a remarkable man. I wonder, do you really know what I have been through?"

"Oh yes. We have watched you and we felt that the assistance you obtained from Michael was quite helpful."

Cubal stopped. "Assistance? I received no assistance. If you watched, then you know that." He paused, glared at the man, then continued, "Indeed, that is a matter about which I am greatly disturbed. Why is it that your god does not take an active role in this war? Is he concerned at all about what this Lucien is doing to his people? Doesn't he know that there are entire cities that have been looted, and the people were all sent to slave worlds?"

Justin's face grew somber. "He knows. And, we know it, Cubal. But, you do not understand."

"Understand? I understand, old one, that millions of people are dying and your god does not stop it. I understand that you say he has the power to stop it, but he does not. Truly, that is something I do not understand." His voice was tinged with anger, and his grey eyes reflected his displeasure.

Cubal folded his arms and stared intently at Justin. His voice softened, and abruptly, he changed the subject. "Why is it that your city survives? And, the place they call Jerusalem? Are there other places like this?"

Justin smiled. "Yes, there are. Our Lord has not abandoned earth as you have suggested. He yet rules. But, Lucifer must be loosed for a short time, to fulfill the Scriptures—to entice the nations. There comes a time of judgment—a final judgment for all."

Cubal started to ask why this god would loose someone so mad with power, but instead, he strode to the table and upended the crystal pitcher, drinking deeply of the water. After he'd finished, he turned to Justin and said, "I do not believe your god has the power you claim he has." Cubal's voice had a hard edge to it and it was obvious that he was still irritated.

Justin smiled. "When you were in the old city there, do you recall stumbling just as you began moving away from the descending soldiers?"

Cubal nodded.

Justin continued, "That stumble was no accident. If your foot had touched the ground at that precise point, you would have found yourself on a faraway world, with no transport devices, and no one, not a single living soul around, and no hope of ever returning. You were tripped intentionally, by Michael."

Cubal remembered that and remembered his astonishment. He was not someone who tripped—*ever*. He was not one to lose his balance, nor stumble. But there, he had stumbled, inexplicably. He stared for a long time at Justin.

"You know, just when I feel I have a grip on you and your religion, and your god, you keep surprising me, keep making me doubt myself, and compel me to rethink things. I do not like it, but I am forced to admit that your story is very plausible, indeed, it is probably true. One such as myself does not trip or stumble, yet I did."

*And Lucien would be that clever, to somehow anticipate my exit point and plant a device such as that.*

176

"Tell me, old one, how is it that this creature Lucien was able to anticipate my moves as he did? I know he has powers, but it would seem he has powers that are akin to those you claim for your god. Can he read minds as you and your people seem to do? Or, can he be in all places as you claim your god can do?"

Justin smiled and shook his head. "No, my friend, he cannot be in all places, nor can he read minds. But, he is a student of the human mind, and he has studied the human species for thousands of years. Also, this creature has many inventions now to assist him. The way he tracked you was with a small pod which he planted on your person when you were with him. Recall the device he gave you, the medallion, the one you left on your bedding at Lucien's abode?"

Cubal nodded and said, "Yes, it was not something someone like myself would ever wear, and although I accepted it and permitted it to be placed in my hands, I did not wear it."

Justin said, "In the ceremony of the placing of that medallion, there was left upon your person a tiny pod which was used to track you. They knew exactly where you were at all times."

Cubal's face showed his astonishment. "I examined my person for such things. There was nothing there. I examined with my touch and my eyes."

"You would not have detected this, Cubal. It cannot be seen by the eye, and it rests attached to your inner garment. The pod is charged so that it will leap from the medallion and onto an article of clothing, and there attach itself."

"When did you know of this?"

Justin's lips curled in a curious little smile and his eyes twinkled as he replied, "When it was planted."

"And you did not warn me? Was it your intention that I perish?"

Justin shook his head. "It was important for you to test Lucien and his ways. There were things you had to learn."

"I could have learned that I was a dead man." The words were spoken matter-of-factly, without emotion. He knew what Justin said was true, that it was important that he had tested those forces. He'd learned much in those brief encounters. It had been a very valuable and productive time, even though death had laid its head on his shoulder. He'd learned that he could survive against Lucien.

Justin was silent, and finally, Cubal shook his head in disgust. "Is there no end to these insidious inventions? How can one escape such devices?"

Justin passed his hand briefly down Cubal's left side and walked to the crystal of water. He dipped his hand into the crystal for a long moment, then declared: "It is gone. Its energies have been eliminated."

Cubal asked, "Is the water deadly to these little pods?"

Justin nodded in agreement. "Water penetrates their mechanism and dissolves them shortly thereafter. Had your inner clothing gotten wet, this device would have ceased to operate."

"I had no time for baths."

Justin laughed. "You may have one before you leave. But, no matter, for though he knows you are here, he cannot attack this place." His eyes grew wistful, then he added, "Not yet, anyway. The time has not yet come."

"You almost seem to yearn for that day."

"Oh, but I do, for in the day that he comes against the saints here and in Jerusalem, our Lord shall appear, and with only his voice, shall destroy all who seek our harm, and will defeat Satan, that is Lucien to you, forever."

Cubal shook his head slowly from side to side, a frown covering his face. He looked up at the man and said, "Yours is a belief I find difficult to accept, Justin. I say that if your god is able to do that, then now's the time for him to speak." In a mocking gesture, with hands held palm upward and his face to the ceiling, he said loudly, "Speak those words, my general and we can end this thing now. I do not care for your war."

Justin was silent.

Cubal took a deep breath, exasperated at the seeming contradictions that came from Justin and this belief system that claimed a god with power to defeat an enemy, but did not. Finally, he said, "Justin, I must wage war with this Lucien creature. I know now that I can defeat his armies, though I must admit that for a time I was very angry with your god, for I thought that I had been lied to about Lucien not being able to come against me directly. Although he did speak directly to me, he did not come against me directly."

"You should leave now, Cubal."

"Leave? To where?"

"You must leave Earth, for your war is out there at this time." Justin pointed up toward the stars. "There is much for you to do there. Blythe awaits your arrival."

Cubal said, "Is this now the will of your god?"

"It is the will of God, yes."

"And how do you propose to place me there?"

"We have a transport device similar to the one owned by the A'rkji race, though ours is superior."

"You have such a device here, in this place?"

Justin nodded. "You must eat and rest, then you must leave. Lucien is enraged that you have escaped him and complains bitterly because you are not one of us, yet you have received assistance."

Cubal laughed, his laughter coming from deep within. "I am sorry, old one. I do not laugh at you, but it amuses me that Lucien would complain about fairness."

"Oh, but he complains all the time. He protests continually to our God about many things."

Cubal's eyebrows raised. "Lucien has actual communications with your god?"

"Yes. That is something God has permitted him."

Cubal shook his head slowly in disbelief. "Why would your god speak to Lucien?"

"You will have to ask God that question some day."

Cubal's right eyebrow arched slightly and he permitted a faint smile to cross his lips. "I shall." He picked a piece of fruit from the table, looked back at Justin and his smile widened into a grin as he added, "If ever I get to meet him."

"You shall. Everyone must meet Him. In God's time, you shall, too." Justin moved away from the table, and before disappearing through the shielded doorway, said, "But now, you must eat and rest yourself. You may wash in the rooms down the hall. Tomorrow, we go to the Journey Room. Then, you must leave."

"I am not inclined to leave."

Justin's eyes narrowed slightly and in his voice, there lay a someberness he'd not heard in the man before. "You may remain here if you choose, but you must not venture outside of this place, lest you die." The way Justin said it made it a declaration, a fact.

"And this is something you are certain about, Justin?"

The man smiled at Cubal, understanding the warrior's heart and his desire to go back into the battle, to live or die. He said softly, "Is there not a saying in your teachings 'To defeat the strong, one must search that strength for its weakness'?"

Cubal's eyebrows raised. "You surprise me, Justin. I would not have thought such writings would have ever come across your eyes. But even so, it is also written in the ways of D'vru that 'the strength of an enemy is measured by his weakness.' I have measured Lucien's weakness in part. But, I must learn more."

Justin nodded and replied, "You will learn more of the creature, as all of the world will learn. But the most important lessons, you have already been taught. You seek the weakness of evil incarnate. It's weakness lies within your own weakness."

Cubal's eyes widened. He opened his mouth to ask the obvious question, then stopped. *I must think on this matter.* He took a small sip of water, then asked, "I know many things I have learned, but what is this most important lesson I have been taught?"

Justin walked to the edge of the lighted doorway and stood framed there. He looked for a long time at the sky outside, then turned to Cubal and said, "Have you not learned that the victory in this war thus far has come because of Messiah, and that in order to win this war against Lucient, you require his assistance?"

The warrior blinked, as he now permitted his thoughts to be accepted as fact.

*Indeed, I would be dead, but for the intervention of the one called Messiah, or someone aligned with him in some fashion.* The thoughts lay there bare, and he accepted them as fact.

Cubal rose, feeling the tension leaving him. He felt as relaxed in this place as he had on Glale. Somehow, he had a feeling of security that was unusual for him to have. He was surrounded by enemies, but here he was in a small bubble of tranquility. It brought a flicker of a smile to his face. He approached Justin, and with a hand extended said, "Justin. I will stay here a little longer and learn more of this Messiah. Bring out that book again."

Justin gripped the warrior's extended hand and said, "You are welcome to stay for a short time, my friend. I will be happy to tell you more of our Messiah and you may continue to read in the Holy Book. It will bring wisdom that will assist you in your war."

Cubal nodded, and said, "I will remain her for a few days, no more than three, will study the book, and will ask you many questions, if that is acceptable to you. Also, if you have a copy of this book somewhere, I would take such a copy with me, for later study, though I would prefer one of smaller size. I must know more of this Lucien creature." He paused, then added, with a smile, "And more about this god-general I am to serve."

Justin returned the smile. "I have already prepared a copy for your journey. It is in a more modern form." He held out a very small, flat object shaped in an oval.

"There is a place in your cloak where this will attach as though it belonged there." He smiled. "Indeed, it actually does belong there. When you wish to read, simply speak the words. If you wish to read in Romans, you will say that word. Or, if you wish to simply read where you left off reading, simply speak the word read."

Justin reached into the left side of the cloak and placed the oval object. "It has now become a part of the cloak and cannot be extracted. Speak the word read."

Cubal said softly, "Read." Instantly a large screen appeared before his eyes and he saw it was the very beginning of the book.

"You may adjust the size of the screen by saying the word smaller or larger." Justin had a large smile across his face. Clearly, he was delighted.

"Is this visible to everyone?"

"Only to you, unless you speak the word visible."

"Good! Then, let me begin the study." He paused as a thought struck him, then asked, "Justin, what about the Crs'tings? Are they behind the weapons of cold and gravity?"

Justin nodded, then replied. "Yes, but it is through their Master, Lucien. He instructs them." Justin paused, closed his eyes for several seconds, then turned his gaze to the open window and said, "They will come soon, warrior. Even now, they prepare for their return to Earth."

The man turned to Cubal, smiled and added, "But, it is so written. They will return from their nest, for God is pulling them home to their destruction."

Then, the two men disappeared through the door and into the brightness of the day, Justin the Teacher already at work, and Cubal, Wearer of the Gold, listening intently, but with measured scepticism.

.

### *The End*

copyright 2011
Voyle A. Glover

\*\*\*\*\*\*\*\*\*\*\*\*\*\*

If you liked this novel, would  you do the author a *huge* favor? It is important to know whether you liked the book and would like to read more of this saga.

If you want more, then it is vital that you go to the Amazon page where this book is located and *make a comment*. That will encourage the author to continue his work on this series. Even better, would you *Tweet* your comments to your friends and recommend it?

*http://millenniumsoldier.com*

www.ingramcontent.com/pod-product-compliance
Lightning Source LLC
Chambersburg PA
CBHW071239130626
46556CB00003B/1081